# THE BOOK OF MAPS

## FORBIDDEN BOOKS, VOLUME IV

DAVID MICHAEL SLATER

LIBRARY TALES PUBLISHING

PRINTED IN THE UNITED STATES OF AMERICA

Published by:
Library Tales Publishing
511 6th Avenue #56
New York, NY 10011
www.LibraryTalesPublishing.com

For general information on our other products and services, please
contact our Customer Care Department at 1-800-754-5016. For tech-
nical support, please visit www.LibraryTalesPublishing.com

Library Tales Publishing also publishes its books in a variety of
electronic formats. Every content that appears in print is available
in electronic books.

ISBN-13: 978-0998333434
ISBN-10: 0998333433

*For Heidi, who gives me direction(s).*

*"In time, those Unconscionable Maps no longer satisfied, and the Cartographers Guild drew a Map of the Empire whose size was that of the Empire, coinciding point for point with it..."*
*~ Jorge Luis Borges*

# PROLOGUE

bbot Augustine looked up from his atlas and saw he had a visitor. A young monk holding a large book was standing at the door staring intensely at the map-covered walls of his study. After reluctantly pausing the heavenly music playing on his phone, Augustine removed the headphones from his massive head and cleared his throat.

"Begging your pardon, Abbot!" the monk blurted, his fair skin flushing. "I am—it is a great honor to meet you—that you have come to us in our trouble. I am—"

"Brother Joe Fausten. I am pleased to see you up and about. Perhaps you have discovered that work is the best medicine for grief."

"Indeed I have," the monk agreed, his blue eyes downcast.

"Let us give thanks that he is in a better place," Augustine advised. "A dreadful accident. Dreadful! I understand the former abbot was something of a mentor for you. You must have impressed him very much to be named assistant librarian at such a young age—and after only a few months of service here at the abbey!"

"I have a passion for research," Brother Joe explained, smiling modestly. Then he looked into the abbot's dark eyes, which were set well into the obese man's fleshy face, and added, "I'm especially interested in the origins of Evil."

"A rich field—of that there is no doubt. This does not prevent you from focusing on your duties here?"

"You have your own personal interests, do you not, Abbot Augustine?" Brother Joe made bold to flick his eyes at the walls.

Augustine studied the monk's earnest pink face a moment, then offered a thick-lipped smile. "Indeed I have," he admitted, chuckling. "Now, what can I do for you tonight?"

Brother Joe looked disappointed by the change of subject, but he answered the question. "I've come to let you know we've finished the inventory," he said. "It was quite an undertaking."

"Wonderful!" Augustine delighted. "Tell me, what did you discover? Come in! Come in!"

The young monk stepped tentatively onto the plush carpet of the softly glowing room. "As you predicted," he said, "there were a number of books missing, as well as a number on the shelves unaccounted for. I am very embarrassed, but I assure you we have not been lax in our—"

"Such has been the case in every abbey I've had the pleasure of taking under my wing," the abbot interrupted. "There is nothing to be ashamed of. The good is in the mending."

"That is most charitable," Brother Joe replied.

"Anything of interest among these un-catalogued books?"

"Not in the library proper, but because you insisted we be total in our vigilance, we examined the safe as well."

"Indeed?" Abbot Augustine's great caterpillar-like brows rose on his expansive forehead. He focused now on the book in the monk's hands, a large leather-bound volume wrapped round with latching straps.

"We use the safe to secure works deemed blasphemous but too important to destroy," Brother Joe explained. "Over time, opinions tend to change, as I'm sure you know."

This received a nod from the abbot, whose gaze stayed locked on the book.

"There was only this one," Brother Joe continued. He lifted the book he'd brought for inspection. "The cover," he said, "seems to have something very much like the symbol you asked us to watch for. I brought it up right—"

The abbot heaved his great bulk forward and grabbed the book from Brother Joe's startled hands. "You may go," he said after settling back into his protesting chair. His head was already down and his finger moving slowly over the emblem impressed on the book's cover. "I thank you for bringing this to my attention," he added without looking back up.

"There was an envelope with it," Brother Joe said, "presumably with details of the book's acquisition. But I didn't take the time to examine the contents because I knew you'd want to see it right—"

"Yes, excellent," Augustine said. "Bring me the envelope. Right away."

"Very well," Brother Joe replied. But he hesitated, rubbing the start of a stubbly goatee.

"What is it, brother?" the abbot asked, looking up now. His voice was kind, but it did not mask his impatience.

"My apologies," said the monk. "But I was wondering—these attacks this past year, all at libraries and bookshops around the world—so many at religious institutions. I must admit some of us are anxious. There are many theories about what is being sought. And who is—"

"Idle chatter," the abbot declared, waving this away. But then he smiled again and added, "Fear not, my son. No one but me is searching for *this* old curiosity. I can promise you that."

"It's just that the nature of the attacks has stirred up some very old fears. We—some of us—thought since—it is believed that you have been sent to some of the sites—that you might know—"

"As I said, Brother Joe, idle chatter. Idle chatter and wayward imaginations. I'm certain your personal interests have not rendered you susceptible to conspiracy theories."

"I'll go retrieve the envelope," Brother Joe said, getting the message. He departed quickly.

When the tiresome child was gone, the abbot looked down again at the prize in his lap. His thick fingers shook as he fumbled with the latches. When they were finally freed, he opened the book and looked inside.

He gasped.

Augustine rolled his chair over to the desk, where he set the book carefully down. Trembling now all over, he lifted the chain with its cross from his neck and set it next to the book. Then he freed another, hidden chain, this one worn under his voluminous robes—a jagged iron crescent.

His talisman.

The abbot willed himself to calm down. He needed to get an email out. Immediately. How long he had hoped to have the privilege and the glory to share this news. So many libraries. So many years. He would need to reveal his name, but so much the better.

His hands were steady now, so he opened his secret account and sent off a simple six-word message: "I have the Book of Maps."

# CHAPTER ONE
## *Officially Over*

A hugely fat man in a brown robe, sprinting full-out, rounded the corner, nearly losing his footing. He staggered, then righted himself and ran on, heading up the opposite sidewalk in the direction of the bookshop. The twins, who were both tinkering with the window display for probably the hundredth time that day, saw him at the same time. They stopped what they were doing and watched. When the man drew near, they could see he was terrified. His face was drenched with sweat and he clutched something: a book. Dexter and Daphna looked at each other for a moment.

It was nearly eleven o'clock on Sunday night, so all the other businesses in Multnomah Village were closed and there were no pedestrians about. The light in the shop evidently attracted the man's attention because, as he passed it across the street, he looked over and saw Daphna and Dexter staring at him dumbly.

A moment later, he was blundering toward them.

"Um, is the door locked?" Dexter asked, but before he had a chance to check, the man burst through it, his eyes kaleidoscopic with fear.

"We don't open 'til tomorrow!" Daphna cried, realizing as she said it how foolish she sounded. But the man—a monk?—stumbled right past her and attacked the store shelves. He began grabbing random books from any which where, only to toss them on the floor after a quick glance at their covers.

"*I'll go get Evelyn,*" Daphna whispered, but as she tiptoed toward the basement steps, the monk grunted with something like satisfaction. He'd pulled a book off the antiques shelf and was looking at it closely. Daphna recognized it—a valuable old account of Portland's underground tunnels. It had latching straps very much like the one the monk ran in with. He was holding them side-by-side now, looking at them together.

"What's going on?" Dexter demanded.

At this, the monk looked over and took in the twins' baffled expressions, but he did not speak to them. Instead, he dropped his book among the others on the floor, then scrambled straight back out of the store with theirs.

That did it for Dexter. They weren't going to be shoplifted mere hours before the Grand Opening. Or shop-traded. Or whatever the heck just happened. "Hey!" he shouted, running outside.

Daphna followed, not so much angry as shaken. Something told her that the year of precious normalcy she and her brother had enjoyed with their adoptive mother was now officially over.

"Stop!" Dexter shouted into a stiff breeze suddenly sweeping the dimly lit street.

To his surprise, the monk obeyed. He reversed course, lurching toward the twins, who stepped back. "Get inside!" he hissed, desperately scanning the street. "Turn off the lights," he added, "and hide!" The twins hesitated, which brought one last warning. "Or you will surely die!"

"Let's go inside," Daphna said, grabbing her brother by the arm. He didn't resist. A black dread was seeping into them both. As the massive monk fled across the street, they hurried back into the shop, turned off the light, and locked the door.

"The attacks," Dexter whispered.

He didn't need to say more. All year they'd been following news of the strange attacks at bookshops and libraries, the disappearance of their caretakers and owners who'd strangely, and disturbingly, left only their clothes behind. There'd been no attacks in the U.S. yet, so Evelyn hadn't gotten too worked up about it.

The monk had stopped on the sidewalk across the street and was looking up. There came a terrible screeching sound, and it made him cower. Just above him, the banner proclaiming "Multnomah Days Parade" began to thrash about. Then it was simply torn from its ties and whipped away like a shot. A windstorm was descending on the Village, and it sounded like a jet roaring down the street. Baskets of flowers hanging from the telephone poles were flung into the air. Then the streetlights began to pop. Crouching at the window, the twins shrank away from the scene, but they could not take their eyes from it.

It was all the monk could do to hold on to a lamppost and not lose the book he took. The winds were ferocious, like the flapping of a million malevolent wings—which is exactly what Dexter and Daphna began to see: black, flapping wings in the thundering dark. And it was suddenly cold, cold enough to penetrate straight through the walls of the shop and halt their hearts. They both knew that sound. They'd both felt that cold when they had fallen into the fissure at Eden's edge, where countless bats had nearly cut them to pieces. They wanted to run now, to call for Evelyn, but they couldn't. Daphna was able only to snatch up her brother's hand.

Suddenly, the wind and flapping stopped. The monk stood on the sidewalk, seemingly paralyzed with fright. A few streetlights flickered weakly, but they shed enough light to illuminate a hooded figure in a flowing white cloak moving toward him in a mist. The figure moved casually, but with terrible purpose.

Both Dexter and Daphna felt their mouths go dry. They were shivering.

The monk dropped the book he'd taken from their store. He lifted something hanging from a chain around his neck and held it up—a curved metal shard of some kind. Then he spun round, pointing it at the apparition now just before him. But the white-clad figure simply reached out, and with long, feminine fingers, took it from him, then tossed it aside where it clinked and echoed ominously on the street.

Its back was to the shop as it lowered its hood, unleashing an avalanche of wild white hair. The monk cried out, but the sound was swallowed almost at once because the thing leapt upon him. That hair, alive and swarming like a thousand bloodless serpents, engulfed both bodies entirely. But seconds later, the monster stepped back. It calmly raised its hood, once again hiding the hair.

The great robe the monk had been wearing fell to the ground over his sandals—empty.

# CHAPTER TWO
## *Damage*

The twins nearly choked. But before they could confirm with each other that what they'd just seen had actually happened, they heard Evelyn coming up the basement stairs.

"Kids?" she called. "Is everything okay? Is there a storm?"

Dexter dove to the foot of the door. *"Don't come up!"* he whispered into the space below it.

"What?" Evelyn asked, though whether because she heard him or didn't hear him wasn't clear.

"It's okay," Daphna said, turning the lights back on. Her voice was hollow, a husk. "It's gone. It picked up the book he swiped from us and just—disappeared with the wind."

Dexter got up on shaky legs. The basement door opened.

"What's happened?" Evelyn asked when she saw the books on the floor. Then she saw the twins' faces and her old eyes narrowed in alarm. "Is something wrong?" She was carrying a stack of books in her bony arms and moved toward the counter to set them down. But no sooner had she done so, she saw the book the monk had dropped.

"What's this?" she asked, picking it up, pale as the kids had ever seen her.

"Outside," Daphna said, pointing, unable to explain any better.

Evelyn walked to the front window and peered outside. Her ancient face, an unfathomable maze of intricate lines, was deeply concerned. A mailbox was on its side in the middle of the road. Flyers previously attached to telephone poles were scattered everywhere. After a moment, Evelyn's normally soft, knowing eyes widened behind her glasses. She gave the book to Dexter, pulled the door open, and stepped outside.

"Don't!" the twins both called, but she was already crossing the street.

The monk's book seemed to be in perfect condition. A strange symbol was impressed on its cover:

The image wavered a bit for Dex, of course, because of his vision problem. He had a name for it now: Scotopic Sensitivity Syndrome. It had to do with his eyes taking in too much light sometimes. "Here," he said, handing the book to Daphna, but she was too focused on Evelyn to look at it closely.

Evelyn was standing over the monk's robe now and seemed to be studying it, but then turned her attention to the metal object lying in the street. She walked over and picked it up. Holding it gingerly, Evelyn studied that too, but only for a moment. Suddenly, she hastened back to the shop as best as she could on her lanky old legs, looking grave.

"We need to leave," she said when she stepped inside. "Now. This very minute." She took the monk's book back from Daphna.

"What's going on?" Dex asked. "Does this have something to do with all those attacks?"

"I'm not sure," was all Evelyn replied. The ever-present calm they'd come to cherish in her was gone. She looked uncertain and afraid, and that, as much as anything, unnerved them.

"What's happening?" Daphna asked, tears leaping to her eyes. "Does this have anything to do with the Book of Nonsense? We destroyed it! We destroyed the Words of Power! Rash is dead! Dad is dead! Mom is dead! *Everyone* is dead! Things have been fine for almost a year!" It sounded like begging. This simply could not be happening again. But it wasn't happening *again*. As awful as the deadly events she and Dexter had endured last year had been, they'd seen nothing like what they'd just witnessed. Now it seemed her nightmares were coming true—nightmares she'd mentioned to no one that forced her to relive that flapping, that awful flapping in the bottomless fissure full of sulfurous vapor. She sometimes thought she smelled that vapor in her waking hours too. Worst of all was dreaming of that laughing, that inhuman laughing they'd heard while falling. It made her feel like each night would be her last.

"Is our father alive?" Dex demanded. "Did he survive the fall too?" It wasn't a stretch to imagine this. Dexter had been suffering nightmares about exactly that since the day it all finally ended outside those Turkish caves, nightmares of falling forever through a noxious wind, nightmares he'd kept to himself because of that laughing, that laughing that sounded like it came from hell—that laughing he heard echo softly sometimes even when he was wide awake.

"Milton—Adam—is dead," Evelyn said. "What has come

here tonight is beyond him. It is beyond me. Now hurry, we must—"

They all heard the wind. It was subdued at first, like a long, fatal exhalation. Dex slammed the lights off. Then they saw the sable wings flowing into the street, hundreds of them moving swiftly and silently, like poisoned black water.

Evelyn, moving silently herself, grabbed the twins and shoved them toward the basement steps. "We'll go out the back," she said, hustling them down the wooden stairs. The spacious room under the shop was unfinished and cluttered with tables straining under heaps of books to be inventoried. Everything their father had in storage. The seeds of a new life they were supposed to begin cultivating in the morning.

Midway through the laden tables, Evelyn stopped and turned to the twins. "Children," she said, "I know I promised I'd be here for you until—"

"No!" Daphna cried, recoiling from the subject she hadn't faced since the one and only time they'd discussed it. With the Book of Life destroyed, Evelyn was withering like a tree sundered from its roots. Signs of decline were obvious: her movements had slowed drastically; her creakiness had increased; her skin had cracked like old parchment. Four or five years was Evelyn's best hope. Daphna had ignored it all.

"What's happening?" Dex roared as rage began to overwhelm his shock at whatever was suddenly destroying everything they'd worked so hard to put back together. Not even *back* together. What they'd built was something they'd never had: a fully functioning family. Even if their time together was characterized almost exclusively by silences, they were safe silences. Dex treasured them because he'd needed time to curl up inside and think—or more truthfully, not to think. They'd provided him with a protective bubble. But that bubble had burst. "It's those attacks, isn't it?"

Evelyn looked helpless. "I've been foolish to have ignored them," she admitted. "I've only wanted to think about you. There is history even I was not privy to."

"But that's impossible!" Daphna protested. "You're *Eve!* The oldest person in the world!"

"Now that's just rude," a woman's voice replied. It was beautiful—nuanced, elegant, and soft. It came from an awful smelling mist that spilled down the stairs.

The twins recognized the sulfurous odor at once. Daphna felt faint. Dexter nearly vomited.

The cloaked figure stood in the basement when the mist dispersed, holding the book the monk had taken, which it tossed to the floor. It was suddenly freezing cold again. "But enthusiasm never respects experience, does it?" the lovely voice added. "I never doubted the trail would lead back to you, children of Adam and Eve—my saviors."

"Who—what *are* you?" Evelyn demanded, stepping in front of the twins. Her voice was strong but strained. Dex and Daphna, both petrified, stared into the darkness under the hood where they could now make out two red eyes over two red lips curled like grinning gashes. Both were horrified that this *thing* knew who they were.

"*Patient* is what I've been," the terrifying figure replied. "*Ready* is what I am."

"I—I don't understand," Evelyn stuttered.

"Of course you don't, old woman," the thing replied. And then it laughed.

The twins' hearts seized at the sound. It was the laughter from the fissure, from their nightmares—a piercing, horrid, inhuman glee.

The stink Daphna had thought she'd been imagining. The laughing Dex thought he'd been crazy to keep hearing.

This thing had been there with them, all year.

"You—you were there," Dex croaked. "In the chasm."

"It was *I* who caused those quakes when those fools returned to die! God's precious pair," the figure sneered. "It is *I* who has unleashed my fury on Eden for centuries!"

"No," Dexter said. He was talking to himself. "No more. There can't be more."

Daphna understood her brother perfectly.

"Give me that, old woman," the figure ordered Evelyn, who was still holding the monk's book, "or I will take the children."

"But we've never seen it before!" Daphna cried, unsure where the courage to speak came from. "That man! He ran into our store with it. He just left it here!"

"She's right," Evelyn confirmed. "This book is no concern of ours." She stepped forward, but did not hand it over, worrying the twins. "You'll want to note one particularly interesting passage," she said instead. Her hand was inside the book, as if marking the page in question.

The cloaked figure moved forward eagerly to see. Evelyn opened the book, and now Daphna and Dexter understood what she was doing. Her hidden hand was clutching the monk's metal shard—and she lunged at the thing's heart with it.

But it reacted with incredible speed. A vicious sweep of its arm sent Evelyn flying off her feet. The book and shard went flying as well.

In the next instant, the thing leapt on Evelyn. Both bodies, now on the floor at Daphna's feet, were already engulfed in a storm of livid hair. Daphna's mind threatened to shut down completely. She didn't know what to do and couldn't think. She wheeled around looking for something, anything. But boxes and books and blinding fear were all she perceived. But then she saw her brother. He was standing directly over the writhing mass of hair, holding the shard like a dagger up over his head.

"Do it!" Daphna cried.

"But I can't tell—!"

*"DO IT!"*

Dexter plunged the point of the jagged crescent into the hair.

For a moment, nothing happened. But then there was a nauseating sound, the sickening wet puncture of teeth piercing flesh.

Evelyn screamed.

Then the thing screamed—an unholy scream—a scream such as the twins had neither heard, nor imagined possible. It attacked their ears like claws. The thing—the monster—flailing and screeching, leapt off its prey, thrashing with the blade in its back under a canopy of wild, whipping hair. As it lashed about, Dexter and Daphna saw teeth—long, jagged yellow teeth clenched in pain. They looked on, transfixed.

Finally, it—she—pulled the shard free and hurled it away.

It landed at Dexter's feet.

Dex picked it up, ready to strike again, but the shard was white hot. He cried out as the flesh of his hand was seared. The moment he dropped it, the metal melted away to nothing.

Daphna, who'd been watching the agonized creature attempt to pull on her hood, turned to her brother when he screamed.

When she turned back, it was gone.

# CHAPTER THREE
## The Book of Maps

"Evelyn!" the twins both cried.

Sprawled on the floor, the ageless woman struggled to breathe. Dark splotches covered her cheeks, and her neck had swollen grotesquely. Daphna and Dexter rushed to her, but she held up a shaky hand that compelled them to stay back.

"Old bone," Evelyn wheezed. "Too weak. To fight it." She fought for air, then gasped out a few more words. "You. Safe. It must not have the book." But she could manage no more.

"Evelyn?" Daphna whined. But the only reply was the sound of gurgling breaths. Horrified, she rushed upstairs for a phone.

Dexter picked up the latched book. "Evelyn?" he tried, but it was obvious she wasn't going to say anything more. He assumed she could hear, but he didn't know what to say. He didn't know where he should look or what he should do. Did she need CPR? He'd skipped class the days they'd learned it!

Thankfully, Daphna leapt back down the stairs. "They're on their way," she said. "I told them it was me, that I was her. I pretended I could barely breathe."

"Why?"

"So they'd think she's alone—so we can get the book out of here. But, Dex, when I said I had blotches on my face and my neck was all swollen up, they got all freaked out and told me not to go near anyone under any circumstance."

"They think it's some disease?" Dex's stomach turned over. "Maybe we better go with them then. What if we have it too?"

Sirens sounded outside.

"Dex," Daphna pleaded, "that mist that stuck to us when we came back from Eden—remember? We set that unspeakable thing free! This is our fault! This is what we get for using Words of Power!"

"But—"

"We can't tell the police that! There is literally nothing true about this situation we can tell them. We're the only ones that can help Evelyn—and ourselves, if we're sick. We need to get out of here and find out what's going on."

Dex conceded, though all he could do was nod since he was nearly hyperventilating at the thought of not being able to breathe.

"Evelyn?" Daphna tried, turning back to her. But there was no response.

The sirens were getting louder.

It felt utterly wrong to leave the poor woman lying there—an unforgivable act—but what choice did they have?

"Don't worry!" Daphna called as she and her brother headed for the basement's outside door. "We promise we'll—!" But she didn't know what they were going to do.

The sirens were nearly upon them now, so the twins did what they could: they ran.

Three minutes later the pair wheeled around the corner, saw their house—and skidded to a halt. A black Cadillac was parked halfway up on the curb in front with its driver's door standing open. A large cross dangled from the rear-view mirror. The garden the twins had recently planted with Evelyn was mostly uprooted.

"Wind," Daphna said, shuddering as she looked at the mangled gardens up and down the street.

A neighbor's fence was down.

Dex was chilled, but now that he wasn't operating entirely on terror, the pain in his hand re-registered and he cried out again. Daphna took the monk's heavy book from him, then grabbed his wrist to get a look at his hand. It was blistering. Without another word, she herded him down the long driveway and in through the back door. She put the book on the kitchen table, then led Dex to the sink, where she turned on a stream of cold water.

Dex stood with his eyes closed, his hand under the soothing flow, for five minutes without saying a word. The cold felt so good. He watched his face in the window for splotching, but it was only red from perspiration. His spiky mess of black hair drooped.

Daphna spent that time digging around in the medicine closet. When she thought Dex was ready, she turned off the water, slathered his entire hand with ointment, then wrapped it with some gauze she'd found. Finally, she made him take aspirin and drink two glasses of water.

Dexter submitted to his sister's ministrations, and with

none of the resentment he surely would have felt most of his life. They'd grown closer this past year. What choice did they have after being orphaned in such an awful way? There was no one—not one human being outside of Evelyn—to share the story with. Who would ever believe that their father had been the first human being ever to live? That Eden was a library, not a garden, and that God had withdrawn from the world to give his beloved creatures dominion over their own lives—to give them Free Will.

It was still too much to comprehend what they'd been involved in. Not that they ever talked about what had happened and what it all meant. What was there to say? Knowing they could was what mattered. It had been enough to start over.

It was a burden, but it was also a bond.

Neither twin had made new friends in eighth grade. Daphna could no longer even remotely relate to kids her age. Her peers seemed so much younger. They always had, but by years, not decades—centuries!—as they seemed to her now.

Dexter was too focused on beating his SSS, as the special education teacher called his "challenge." He had Dex reading under different types of lights and with various colored plastic sheets over his books, some of which sometimes helped steady the letters on their pages and hold off the brain-crushing headaches reading gave him. His sister helped him with his homework every night, but it was still an ordeal, especially because he insisted on writing out his assignments—even though his teachers said he could use dictation software if he wanted to. Grades had come only a few weeks ago. He'd managed a C+ average the whole year, with no modification of his grades, which he also refused. Daphna acted like his mother, she was so proud. She was so pleased, in fact, that Dex didn't have the heart to tell her how pathetic he felt.

The twins both reflected on their new relationship as Daphna treated Dexter. It seemed they were all each other had. Again.

"Did you see the big cross hanging in that car out there?" Daphna asked, cleaning up.

Dex leaned toward the window in the living room to get a look at the abandoned vehicle beyond. "I see it now," he said.

"That monk must have been looking for Dad. I bet he came here, then had to run from that *thing*—and then came past the store. But I guess he didn't actually know Dad, or didn't know him very well, or he'd have known he was dead."

Dexter nodded. His hand felt significantly better, but it still hurt like crazy. "But why did he want to give dad that book? Was he selling it?"

"Good question."

"And why does that—*thing* want it?"

"We need to find out," Daphna said. She thought a moment, then added, "I guess it didn't know Evelyn was Eve—*is* Eve. It must have assumed Mom was Eve, since she fell with Dad, back in Eden. Dex, that monster has been free all year!"

"The attacks," Dex said. Then he added, "Evelyn. She'll be okay? Do you think we killed it?"

"I hope so," Daphna said. "You certainly hurt it. Dexter, you saved Evelyn's life, *all* our lives. I was useless. Completely useless." Daphna's eyes welled up. "I can't think when there's violence, Dex. I just can't."

"Daphna," Dex said, "you thought your way out of being strangled to death last year."

"Yeah, that's true. I'm such a crybaby."

"What *was* it?"

"I don't know, Dex. Something evil." Daphna thought she'd learned that pure evil didn't exist, that the awful things that happened in life were the results of misunderstandings—misunderstandings that could, at least in theory, be remedied. Over the past year, this belief had allowed her to pack her fears about the world into a neat little box and set it on a shelf in the back of her mind. But now that box had been ripped open and every terror inside was streaming free. It was just like that Greek myth about Pandora.

"What are we going to do?" Dex asked. The thought that evil, real Evil, really existed, was no shock to him. That something was fundamentally wrong with a random world abandoned to its own devices was not a revelation.

"I don't know," Daphna moaned.

"Let's look at the book."

Daphna raised a brow, but did not comment on this unprecedented suggestion from her brother. Instead, she followed him to the kitchen table and sat down in front of the strange, boxy volume. Both of them just stared at it, afraid to open another devastating chapter in their tumultuous lives. But some ominous page had already been turned in their story—and if there was one thing they'd learned so far for sure, it was that happy endings didn't write themselves.

Daphna, having two functional hands, pulled the book over and set to opening the latches, which worked like belts attached to the cover. When they were unfastened, she took a quick glimpse into her brother's mottled green eyes—the same eyes she saw in the mirror every day—then turned over the cover.

On the page lying before them was a map, unrecognizable both in its antiquity and because strange lines, drawings, and symbols overlaid it here and there.

"*Oh, my gosh,*" Daphna gasped. She looked at Dexter. "It's moving."

"Like the Book of Knowledge?" he asked. To him it looked like a crumpled piece of colorful graph paper.

"Yes. No. Not exactly," Daphna said. "The maps aren't changing. They're shifting around, very slowly—to show all the angles, I think." Daphna flipped through some pages and found the same astonishing effect on each one. Maps of all sorts seethed inside the book. Some seemed continental, but others were as detailed as road maps. Some appeared to be political or climatological, others topographical, and those actually rose out of and sank into the pages. The overall effect was to make the book seem to contain the whole living, breathing world.

"*It's incredible,*" Daphna whispered. "I think there are tiny little points of light in some spots. I wonder if they're indicating something."

Dexter ran down to his room, grabbed some colored overlays from the mess on his desk and rushed back up. Daphna watched him lay one at a time over the page she'd been gaping at, but she could see by his darkening expression that none of them did much to help.

"We're burning it," Dex declared. "Right now. We're not going through this again."

It was obvious why Dex's thoughts had turned in this direction, but he was absolutely right. "Okay," Daphna agreed. Only, I better handle the fire."

Daphna got up and fetched a starter log from the crate next to the living room fireplace, set it inside, and had it burning in seconds. She took the book from Dex and set it on top, then buried it completely with balled up newspaper and real sticks and logs. There was a mini-inferno going in no time. Then she and Dex—as if the past eleven months had never happened—sat down to watch yet another impossible book burn.

After a few minutes, Daphna looked at her brother. He was nearly as pale as Evelyn had gotten after being bitten. She, herself, was nearly out on her feet, too, as it was past midnight and all her adrenaline was gone. "You think we're safe going to sleep?" she asked.

"At the moment," Dex replied, "I'm too tired to care."

Daphna was too tired to propose—anything else, actually—so after she and Dex watched the fire for a minute or so more, they went off to bed.

\*     \*     \*

Dex hardly slept. The pain in his hand came and went in waves and forced him to take more aspirin every few hours. But even when it took effect, he lay awake staring at the diffuse light thrown off by the lamp he'd been leaving on every night.

As was all too often the case, his thoughts turned toward resentment. He resented having SSS, a problem never intended for him—a problem he didn't deserve. He resented having to live in a world full of problems nobody asked for and nobody deserved. Most of all, he resented the loss of the incredible powers he'd had for such a short, sweet time—powers that had wiped away a lifetime of feeling defective. Powers that made him feel like a god.

On top of that, what he and his sister had accomplished last year seemed to recede farther and farther into insignificance every day. No one knew what they'd done. No one knew what had almost happened. And now there was something worse out there, something he didn't stand a chance against. For whatever reason, he knew he hadn't killed it, and he knew he'd be seeing it again. And he knew it would be the end of him.

Eventually, Dex must have fallen asleep, because he woke up at six, clearheaded enough to realize how stupid they'd been for leaving themselves unprotected all night in the first place anyone with half a brain would look for them. After dragging on some jeans and the T-shirt Evelyn had designed for the Grand Opening—it said "Paradise Bookshop" and had a picture of a tree bearing books instead of apples—he opened the invisible little door to the storage space under the basement steps. It was invisible now because Evelyn had helped him wallpaper over it to match the walls on both sides. It never had a knob, but popped open when you pushed on it hard enough where it latched. The best part was that she never once asked him why he wanted it that way, so he never had to explain. In fact, she'd laughed when she saw the ankle-deep junkyard inside and called it his treasure trove.

Evelyn was the opposite of the twins' poor mother, who'd pried desperately into their every thought and deed. Evelyn was content to listen, and she had a way of listening that made the twins feel like whatever they told her was the most important thing in the world. Not that Dex really could have explained his feelings anyway. He'd lost his last secret place, the Clearing in the woods of Gabriel Park—that was part of it—but also, he suddenly realized, he must have figured it might come in handy some day to have a hiding place.

Dex grabbed his penlight, which hung on a nail, and used it to help locate what he needed: the switchblade he'd confiscated last year from one of the many people who'd tried to kill him. He tucked it into his back pocket. Dex almost tossed the light into the mess, but thought the better of it and hung it back on the nail. Then he headed upstairs.

\*　　　\*　　　\*

Daphna slept poorly as well. She wasn't so much afraid as furious, furious that what she'd seen had no place in a world she'd come to comprehend this past year. Unlike her brother, who inexplicably didn't seem interested in the subject at all—even given his horrible eye problem and history of academic avoidance—Daphna had done massive amounts of research on pretty much every religion on the planet, even including loopy new age types and the creepy kinds that spend their time trying to summon evil spirits.

She'd been surprised to discover that some mystics in just about all religions seemed to believe pretty much the same thing: God was ultimately somehow gone, unreachable, untouchable, unknowable. She'd learned that if people devoted themselves to years of study and practice, they'd come to this fact and not only accept it, but find comfort in it. This was extremely reassuring.

But now she had to reconsider everything.

She got up early, showered, and threw on some jeans and Eveyln's store T-shirt. Then she brushed her increasingly unwieldy bob at the mirror, thinking how much she really did look like Teal lately—cruel, popular Teal. She'd often dreamed of *being* Teal when she was still an envious little wannabe.

\*　　　\*　　　\*

Dexter was coming through the kitchen, so Daphna came out to meet him in the living room. They smiled to see that they were twins.

Inside the fireplace was a mountain of ash.

"Good," Dex sighed. "No matter what happens, we weren't stupid or selfish this time."

"Exactly," Daphna concurred. She'd taken up a poker and was jabbing it into the ash. "Uh, oh," she said, "some of it might be left."

Dex squatted down on the hearth as Daphna swept the poker toward him. An ashy rectangular lump emerged from the heap. After making sure he wasn't going to burn off his other hand, Dexter picked it up and shook the ashes free.

The book was unscathed.

# CHAPTER FOUR
## Gifts

"What now?" Dexter asked after his sister re-wrapped his hand with fresh gauze and lectured him about the need to re-dress the wound every day. How she knew these things was beyond him. The book was sitting between them on the kitchen counter.

Before Daphna could say, "I don't know" one more time, a car—a stretch limousine—screeched to a halt directly in front of the house. Four large men in blue, papery-looking coveralls, the kind with built-in gloves and boots, jumped out. They all wore masks made of the same material, along with goggles, over their faces, making them look like workers from a nuclear facility. Except they were all also wearing what looked like red silk scarves around their arms.

One went to inspect the monk's abandoned Cadillac. Another had a large canvas bag and scattered something small and granular, like seeds, on the yard. The other two crouched on either side of the limo. They had some sort of strange guns—crossbows?—and they aimed them in sweeping arcs around the yard.

The twins exchanged panicked expressions.

"Under the steps," Dex whispered.

Daphna grabbed the book and, shaking, followed her brother down to his room. He popped open the storage door and they clambered inside. It had only just clicked shut again when they heard the door forced open upstairs.

"At least we locked it this time," Dex whispered, but Daphna pinched him hard—nearly hard enough to make him call out. No matter what she'd managed last year, she was terrified about the prospect of another violent scene. And it was impossible to sit anywhere without something jabbing her. The space was as dark as a coalmine, and nearly as suffocating, with a terrible, almost electric energy. The air inside positively vibrated with tension—Daphna could practically see it vibrating. It was the caves. She was reliving the caves.

Footsteps hammered on the floors upstairs, making the

twins' hearts batter their chests.

Louder crashes followed—the sounds of objects being turned over, swept off surfaces, and emptied out of drawers. Finally, the footsteps came down the stairs directly over their heads. Whatever the men were scattering outside was now being spilled down the wooden steps. It sounded like a waterfall.

"Nobody down here, neither," someone said amidst similar ransacking and spilling sounds in Dex's room. His voice was muffled by his mask. "That Abbey," he complained, "now this? Boss is gonna go ape if they burned it."

"Think the Guild got 'em?" someone replied.

"I don't get paid to think. Let's get out of here. Cover me. And I don't care how crazy he is—don't forget the proper target."

"Got it."

The men headed back up the steps, and in quite a hurry by the sound of it. A moment later, all was quiet.

Dex made a move to open the door, but Daphna yanked his arm back. She made them sit in silence for a solid ten minutes before letting them climb out. She'd nearly squeezed the Book of Maps to dust in there, but it appeared undamaged. Dex closed the switchblade and tucked it away behind his back while she examined the book.

The ransacked version of Dexter's room wasn't so much of a change, even covered in what was in fact some kind of seed, but seeing the state of the upstairs was too much for Daphna. How could they do so much damage in so little time? A life, an entire family's life, lay in shambles: books, picture frames, office supplies, every dish, glass and utensil, linens, papers, toiletries, cleaning supplies, games, lamps, potted plants, entire drawers, half the books she'd used for research this past year—everything was everywhere, and covered in seeds.

The scene—his house turned upside down—was too surreal for Dex to accept, so he didn't accept it. "It stinks in here," he said, slumping onto the living room couch, which had been slashed.

Daphna finally noticed as well. The smell wasn't bad, but it was powerful.

"What is it?" Dex asked. "Smell's like—spaghetti?"

Daphna sank down onto the floor amidst the debris and picked up a handful of seeds from the top of a photo album. "Poppy seeds," she said. But there was something else mixed in. She put a handful to her nose. "And garlic," she added.

"Poppy seeds and garlic? What's it for?"

"How should I know?" Daphna snapped. She opened up the photo album. At least the pictures were all there. She thought she'd lost them once when they'd be taken off to Turkey, and if anything happened to them permanently it would be the final blow, no matter that she'd memorized each and every one. Daphna knew it was unhealthy, but she couldn't stop herself. Every day she spent time staring at the pictures of the woman who'd cared for her, reliving the scenes as if she'd always known Latty was not her housekeeper and caretaker, but her actual mother.

It was no small task to revise a life.

The genuine history she didn't have with her mother ate at her every day, and Daphna's inability to apologize for how distant she'd been during their last year together drove her nearly mad. How could she never have somehow known, deep down inside? It felt like a failure of character. Latty, Sophia, had lived thanklessly for her and Dexter, and then she had *died* for them—thanklessly as well. The least Daphna could do was remember her.

So she stared at the pictures until they told a different story, a story about a mother and daughter who shared everything, a mother and daughter who were best friends. And when she could stare no longer, Daphna imagined pictures that weren't there, albums' worth, that proved it all. Sometimes she worked on her father, too, but it was harder. As she flipped through the album now, her meager defenses fell away, and the tears began to flow.

Dexter watched his sister, once again completely at a loss for words. He was vaguely ashamed, but at least he didn't feel like teasing Daphna—though that might be in order if it stopped her creepy obsession with those pictures. At least once a week he'd go to say something to her in her room, only to find her spaced out staring at the albums, sometimes at entirely empty pages. Most of the time he just walked away without her even knowing he'd been there. "What was that?" he asked, spotting a strange shot as Daphna flipped a page. Speaking of empty—

"What?" Daphna asked, oddly calmed by the prospect of conducting a conversation having nothing to do with the catastrophes at hand.

"That—there—what is that? What are you doing?"

Daphna smiled at the photo. It was taken at the Portland Art Museum when she was in sixth grade. She was standing in a gallery staring at a wall, at a faded square where a painting had once hung. "I remember that," she said. "Mom took the picture 'cause I was so fascinated. We had a memorable time together that day."

Dex let that bizarre comment pass. "You were fascinated by a blank space on the wall?"

"By the possibilities," Daphna explained. She supposed she'd always known something was missing. "She teased me," Daphna added, "but it turned out to be a test."

"A test?"

"A psychology student was there, timing how long people looked at the missing painting. He came over and told me that most people stared at the spot longer than they looked at any actual painting. He said people are intrigued by what's not there more than what is. I stared the longest."

"That's weird," Dex said, though he was tempted to ask how intriguing she found the empty space that was now their lives. Instead, he paced into the kitchen. "I don't get any of this," he said in response to his own thoughts. "Hey, what's this?" There was a business card on the kitchen counter sitting atop a dollar bill. And unless he was mistaken, which was always possible when he looked at money, it was a hundred. Dexter took them to Daphna, who got up to take a look.

"Where'd you get a hundred dollar bill?" she asked. "Hey, there's writing on it. It says, 'A Gift.'" Daphna looked at the business card. "There's a phone number on one side of this," she said, "and it says, 'An Offer,' underneath. Wow," she added, "fancy paper." Daphna flipped it over. "And there's a dollar amount on the back. A *big* dollar amount."

"How big?"

Daphna didn't reply at once. She seemed to be counting something on the card. When she finished, she looked up and said, "One billion."

"Did you say *billion?* With a *B?*"

The twins, according to Evelyn, were set for life based on money left to them by their mother, but the bank had been giving them trouble trying to verify the accounts, which had apparently changed hands once a generation for many generations in somewhat irregular ways. Dex and Daphna had no doubt their mother's many identities was the source of the irregularities. They'd been allowed access to a decent monthly stipend while the matter was being investigated, which was enough to encourage Evelyn to leave her job at the Home. The bookstore was the back-up plan.

"Yeah, with a *B,*" Daphna confirmed. The phone rang right next to her. She grabbed it. "Hello?"

"They *are* there, you idiots!" someone barked. "Turn around!"

Daphna slammed the phone down. "I'm sorry!" she cried, her eyes gone wild. "I'm sorry! I'm sorry!"

"*What?*"

"They're coming back! I thought it could be Evelyn! I—I wasn't thinking! I'm so sorry!"

"Let's go," Dex said, leaning to see out the front window.

Daphna grabbed her shoulder bag, which was hanging on the laundry room doorknob, and stuffed the Book of Maps into it. Then she followed her brother outside, ready once again to run for her life.

But Dexter ran to the monk's Cadillac instead. "The keys are still inside," he said, peering in.

"You can't be serious."

But he was already climbing into the driver's seat. And now the ignition was on.

"Dex!" Daphna cried, standing next to the door. "They'll see the car is gone. They'll come after us."

"They'll come after us anyway. Wouldn't you rather be in a car?"

"But you can't drive! Where are we going to go?"

Dex closed his eyes. "It doesn't matter!" he shouted. "We'll go—find this Abby person they mentioned. She's probably a book dealer!"

Daphna's face went blank for a moment, but then she hurried around the car and climbed in. "Go," she said. "And do not—I repeat, do *not*—get us killed."

But Dexter was gifted when it came to the mechanical. He could take anything apart and put it back together. He instinctively knew how things worked. So why not operate an automobile? No, the logic didn't exactly follow, but Dex didn't care. With a single effort he put the car into reverse and backed off the curb. Then he put it in drive and got the car moving forward.

They'd gone a few hundred feet when the limousine careered around the corner in their rearview mirror, skidded sideways, then screamed toward them.

"Dexter!" Daphna shrieked, craning her neck around.

Just then the air was filled with sirens. What seemed inches from their rear bumper, the limousine executed an incredible one hundred and eighty degree spin and was suddenly gone down a side street. Somehow, Dexter kept going. As he managed to negotiate the corner, three police cars and an ambulance roared past.

"They're looking for us," Daphna realized. "Keep going! Good. Okay. *Oh, God.* Good. Good. Turn right here. No, *right!*"

Dex wheeled one direction, then the other, but made the turn, though he drove over the curb. His foot wouldn't hold steady on the accelerator—the car was jerking forward and back—but they were moving. "Why right?" he asked when his heart stopped threatening to implode. "Where are we going?"

"*Abbey,*" Daphna gasped.

"You know who she is?"

"Look out!"

Dex had lost his concentration for a moment and nearly crossed into the oncoming lane. "Sorry," he said.

"It's not a person. It's *abbey,* like a place with—"

"Monks!"

"Exactly. The Mount Angel Abbey. It has a world famous library of ancient books. *Religious* books. I've been there with Dad a few times. *Red light!*"

Dex slammed on the breaks. Daphna hit the dashboard, Dexter the steering wheel. They'd forgotten to put on their seatbelts, an oversight they corrected immediately.

The light turned green.

"Okay, left and up the hill," Daphna instructed, flexing her wrists, which had taken the brunt of her collision. "I can't believe we're doing this."

Dexter headed up the hill. He was driving slowly, and not much more smoothly. Anyway, he was driving. No one seemed to be following them.

"Okay, up there, turn right at the top," Daphna directed. Dex flipped on the signal. "There! No, up a bit! The highway entrance! There!"

"Okay, okay," Dex said. "I got it." He eased the car around the corner and onto the entry ramp. Carefully, he merged with traffic and gradually brought the car up to speed.

# CHAPTER FIVE
## *Abbey*

"Does it hurt your hand to steer?"

"Now that you mention it," Dex said, "yeah. A lot."

"Watch out!"

Dex had drifted across lanes again. "Sorry," he said. "You keep distracting me."

"I think it's about a half hour away," Daphna said, trying to keep calm. Riding in a car being driven by her not-quite-fourteen-year-old brother at sixty miles an hour violated every principle she believed in—that is every principle ever conceived about not being an idiot and getting yourself killed. "Maybe there's a map in here," she said, trying to ignore her instincts for self-preservation. She opened the glove compartment and looked inside.

"Why don't you just try that book?"

"Keep your eyes on the road!"

That was sound advice. Dex didn't want to make his sister panic—any worse, that is—but it was all he could do to keep from crashing. Not because he couldn't handle the car but because it was hard to tell exactly how far away things were, like that corner he drove over.

"Can't you see?" Daphna cried, suddenly realizing the sheer depth of her foolishness.

"I'm okay," Dex said. "Just help me when we have to make a turn. I won't try to pass anyone."

"I don't believe this," Daphna groaned. "Why am I letting myself be driven by a blind person with a mangled hand and—oh, yeah—no driver's license!"

"I'm not blind," Dex retorted. "And it's because you prefer probable death to certain death."

Daphna reluctantly agreed, so she began fishing around in the glove compartment again. Her fingers discovered something intriguingly hard and rectangular, so she pulled it out. "Dex! Look! No don't! Pull over! Take this exit! Here!"

Dex swerved onto the exit ramp they were just passing, which drew angry honks from the car behind him. He slowed to a crawl until he reached the red light at the end, which drew more horn blasts.

"Go left," Daphna said, thinking all they needed today was a road rage incident. "There's a gas station over there."

Dex made the turn, then a right at another light, then eased the car into the station. He didn't even try to fit into a parking space, but rather just stopped where nothing else was around.

"Look!" Daphna was holding up a fancy new cell phone. "Does it have power?"

Daphna pushed the on button. After a few moments, the screen lit up. "Yep!" she said. "Hold on, I'm getting directions to the abbey." The phone rang—a church bells ring tone—while Daphna typed. She ignored it. A minute later, she had what she needed. "Got it," she said. "I was right. We'll be there in about half an hour. Let's go before something else goes wrong."

"Like me dying from starvation," Dex said.

"Me too. I'll run into the store." Daphna jumped out, digging into her jeans for a few crumpled bills, one of which was the hundred.

"That oughta do," Dex told her through the window.

Daphna came back looking cross. "They wouldn't take it," she groused, climbing back in. But she had a couple of candy bars, which she and her brother made short work of.

Satisfied, Dex headed back out onto the highway without incident. Fortunately, the entry was right there. He was already getting more comfortable working the accelerator and brakes. As he got back up to speed, he allowed himself a moment of pride for what he was pulling off.

"Dex, what happened?" Daphna said, finally able to sit back and relax at least a little bit. "What was that thing? What was that hair? It was like Medusa or something. Did you see her teeth?"

"Don't talk," Dexter said. "I'll crash."

"Okay."

"Oh, no."

"What?"

"Don't look," Dex warned. "There's a police car behind us."

Daphna looked. A cruiser was directly behind them. The cop driving it looked right into her bugging eyes when she spun round. She shoved herself back into her seat.

"Am I speeding?" Dex asked out of the side of his mouth, as if they could be heard.

*"You're going too* slow," Daphna whispered.

Dex sped up a bit, his knuckles white on the wheel.

"Our seatbelts!" Daphna cried.

They'd forgotten again. Carefully, the twins reached over and put them on.

"What are we going to do?" Daphna pleaded when hers clicked in. "We can't just order him to leave this time." Over the school year, Daphna hadn't thought too much about the incredible powers she'd possessed when she could speak the First Tongue. Once she'd given up her immature obsession with the popular crowd, there never really seemed a need. But right now, there was a need for Words of Power. There was definitely a need now.

The police siren suddenly sounded. Red lights splashed into the car, shocking the twins like a bucket of blood. Daphna screamed. Dex swerved back and forth.

The police car swung around into the passing lane, pulled up next to the twins—and then sped away.

Dexter had to stop on the shoulder to settle down.

Daphna needed the time too. When she finally managed to stave off the panic attack, she collapsed against the dashboard. "Why, Dexter?" she whined with her face in her arm. "What did we ever do to anyone? Why does this keep happening to us?"

"Right now," Dex said, "it's not happening to us. It's happening to Evelyn. And we need to find out exactly *what* the 'what' is."

"Right," Daphna agreed, sitting up. "You're right. But that ambulance—what if we're sick and contagious? What if we're out here spreading around some terrible disease?"

"Do you feel sick?"

"No," Daphna admitted. "But your hand—there was blood on that shard, right? It must be dangerous if it got that thing hot enough to melt."

"Yes," Dex admitted. "I'll turn myself in if I get any symptoms. *Okay?*"

"We'll *both* turn ourselves in if *either* of us gets symptoms," Daphna said. "We have to stick together no matter what. Okay?"

"Fine. Okay."

"We better get going."

"Right." After a glance over his shoulder, Dex pulled back onto the highway and got them back on their way.

The phone rang again, but Daphna ignored it, reaching instead into the bag at her feet. She opened the hefty Book of Maps on her lap, hoping to keep her mind off the road. As before, the pages teemed with moving maps, some of which looked much more modern than the ones they'd looked at before. These were covered with unintelligible marks and symbols. Upon closer inspection, Daphna could see some were drawings of monsters. Others were icons of pillars and doors and intricate compass roses. She began flipping through the pages, all of which had pretty much the same dizzying displays of ancient, exotic imaginary, and even some vaguely familiar lands. Pinpricks of light appeared here and there. But then she noticed something else.

"These pages are incredibly thin," Daphna said, trying to turn a single leaf rather than random chunks. She got hold of one that seemed impossibly thin when she lifted it. Like the finest tissue paper, it was nearly translucent. "There must be thousands," she said. "They aren't numbered though. I can't believe they don't tear right out." She gave one a tug.

"Well, they don't burn, either," Dex pointed out.

"Hey," said Daphna after turning over a larger section. "There's a bookmark in here. The page has writing on it. I think it's a story of some kind."

Dex glanced over at the page, but only for a second. "Looks like chicken scratch with string laying all over it to me."

"String?"

"Or white lines. I get that a lot."

"You mean like running up and down, between words?"

"Kinda, yeah."

"I see that sometimes," Daphna said. "Like when I've been reading too long and let my eyes un-focus on a page. Sometimes, if a whole bunch of lines all have a space in the same place—it looks like a white line going down the page."

"That's pretty much it," Dex agreed. "But crazier."

"The story is in English," Daphna said, "but I can't read in the car. I'll get sick. I'll look it over at the abbey." She closed the book, making sure the bookmark stayed in place.

As he drove, Dexter forced himself to concentrate, fixing his eyes on the road. The church bells kept chiming from the phone, but the twins kept ignoring it. Daphna watched the GPS track their movement, which was fascinating. "This is really incredible," she said. "It even has our longitude and latitude coordinates. They change when we move. Tell me this isn't like magic."

Dex didn't reply, so Daphna kept quiet, watching the screen.

Twenty minutes later, she was ready to navigate. "Okay, it

says go left at Newberg Highway. It's 214. Never mind—there! Turn that way, right there past that—Okay—okay—*Now!*"

"Got it," Dex said.

Daphna led him through the rest of the directions, calling out the best moment to turn. They clipped a few curbs, but managed not to crash.

Ten minutes later they were turning onto Abbey Drive and following it up onto a hilltop. The road wound into a parking lot where Dex stopped the car and let out the biggest sigh of his life.

"That's the monastery," Daphna said, letting out a fairly large sigh as well, "the building with the red sloping roofs. Over that way is the guesthouse. That's the library. I guess we should go there."

Dexter released his seatbelt and climbed out of the car. Daphna tucked the monk's phone into her bag with the book and met him on the sidewalk. The twins just stood there looking around the well-tended grounds. Everything was in summer bloom. Trees were arranged just so, hedges were groomed to perfection. The grassy field hosting the quiet buildings around it was a radiant green.

"This place is nice," Dex said. "Peaceful." He was thinking of the Clearing again.

"So quiet," Daphna said, looking around. "Where is everyone?"

The innocent question suddenly cast the silence in a new light. A dark fear settled over the twins.

They looked down.

On the ground between them was a pair of sandals and an empty brown robe.

# CHAPTER SIX
## Brother Joe

The twins wheeled around, ducking and scanning for flapping black wings. Slowly it dawned on them that robes were lying here and there on the paths and fields in eerie, forlorn heaps.

The silence was now deafening.

Daphna grabbed her brother's hand.

"It's okay," Dex said. "No one's here. This is what he was running from—and what followed him."

"To us."

"He was looking for Dad."

"Why?"

"That's what we're here to find out, isn't it?"

"Let's go to the library. Fast. I don't think we should stay here." Daphna led the way from the sidewalk onto a concrete path, but then decided just to cut across the lawn toward the long, low brown structure.

The building itself didn't look like anything special, but Daphna knew it was nothing less than a cathedral. The moment she stepped inside, she completely forgot she was afraid for her life.

The library was all circles, like a nautilus. It was multi-leveled, with concentric rings of shelves and desks that seemed to wrap around her in a glorious, inspirational blur. A large curved section of the ceiling had been carved out, allowing a line of windows to cast natural light over the whole interior. Colors were muted, but in no way boring: rich browns, creamy whites, soft grays, broken here and there by brighter hues among the books that seemed somehow to rotate three hundred and sixty degrees around. The entire space exuded an aura of eternal contemplation. It was one of the most beautiful things Daphna had ever seen. The Library at Eden couldn't have been much finer.

This was all lost on Dexter, of course, who was looking at—a library. Though they didn't by definition fill him with revulsion anymore, it was still just a fancy pile of books, any one of which would probably take him an eternity to read. While his sister stood there slobbering, he walked around, trying doors along the perimeter. They opened into offices, all of which might be worth searching, though for what he had no idea.

When Dex turned the knob on the door across from the main desk, he heard something, a sudden movement in the room. He stepped back and waved to Daphna. He had to hiss to get her to snap out of her reverie, but she hurried over. *"Someone's in there,"* he whispered.

Daphna twisted her wrist back and forth with a questioning look. Dex nodded. Then he opened the door.

"Lord—Please!" someone screamed. "Wait! Please! Let me speak!" It was a small man, a young-looking monk with a scruffy goatee, kneeling on the floor. His head was bowed, and he was holding a cross up over it with his arms extended. He was apparently too terrified to realize he had it upside down.

"Ah, it's okay," Dex said. "We're from Portland—"

"We're visitors," Daphna added. "It's safe." Something—her pathological perfectionism no doubt—made her want to mention the cross, but she held her tongue.

The young man looked up, his eyes bottomless wells of fear. At the sight of the twins, he collapsed, evidently overcome with relief. A moment later, he got up, slowly, tucking the cross under his robe and trying to gather himself. The twins took the opportunity to look around the little room. The walls were covered with maps, most of which were dotted with pins. They looked at each other to note this. Then they turned their attention to the mess that buried the rest of the room. Books were on the floor, drawers opened, papers strewn everywhere.

The monk had walked to the door and was poking his head out to scan the library. When he saw the robes heaped on the floor, his eyes got large. "Gone!" he yelped. Then he walked unsteadily to the large, leather desk chair and collapsed into it.

"What happened?" Dexter asked, though he had a pretty good idea.

"Last night," the monk said, "a few minutes after I gave the abbot a book I discovered—I'd come back with some related materials he requested. That's when the winds came. He told me to hide in his office and lock the door and not to come out no matter what. Then he left. Not long after, the screaming started. I'm sorry—I am Brother Joe, an assistant librarian here."

"Have you been in here since yesterday?" Daphna asked,

concerned but also pleased to learn of the monk's job.

He nodded.

"You need food!"

"The abbot kept a supply," Brother Joe said. "He will forgive me for partaking of it." He looked through the door into the library again and said, "I—I don't know what happened here." His voice was fragile. "It came so close. It came so close—I could *feel* it—the cold." Brother Joe leaned forward and lowered his head.

The twins didn't know what to say. They'd never met a monk before, let alone a traumatized one. In the end, they needed answers more than they needed to be proper. "The abbot," Daphna said, "he came to Portland—we think to talk to our father about a rare book. Probably the book you discovered. Our dad was a bookscout."

"The abbot—" Brother Joe asked, "is he—?"

The twins didn't know how to break the news. Finally, Dexter said, "The wind—it found him."

Brother Joe lowered his head again and softly spoke something that might have been a prayer. Then he looked up and said, "I'd only just met Abbot Augustine, but he was a legendary figure in the Church. He'd been with us a month or so, since our beloved former abbot, who was like a father to me, passed away. You said your father *was* a bookscout?"

"He passed away too," Daphna said.

"I'm sorry to hear that," said Brother Joe. "I hope the circumstances were not too trying for you."

"Oh," said Daphna, who hadn't planned on continuing a conversation about it. "Well, there was an accident."

"I'm truly sorry for your loss," Brother Joe said, quietly. "There was an accident here as well. In the basement. The former abbot always had trouble operating the electronic shelves. They move together and apart to provide space."

The twins shuddered at the thought of what such an accident must have looked like.

Brother Joe was slowly recovering his wits. "So, the abbot found you instead of your father?" he asked. "Did he give you the book?"

After a quickly exchanging look, the twins both said, "No."

"We're trying to figure out what it is, though," Dex said. "Do you know?"

"I'm afraid not," Brother Joe said.

"Do you have any idea why the abbot would bring it to our father?" Daphna asked.

"There was an envelope with the book—the information

I brought to the abbot. It likely had details of the book's acquisition. If your father dealt in rare books, maybe the abbey originally obtained it from him and the abbot had some questions about its origin."

"Can we see the envelope?" Dexter asked.

"I'm sorry," Brother Joe said. "It seems the abbot took it with him."

"Is there any way to know if our father has ever been here?" Dex wondered. "On business, I mean?"

"We had to sign in when we visited together," Daphna said. "Do you keep records of everyone who comes?"

"As a matter of fact," Brother Joe said, "part of a reorganization we've just completed for the abbot was entering the contents of all our visitor logs into a database."

"Can we see it?" Daphna asked.

Having a task seemed to help Brother Joe recover even more. His color was normal now. He turned the chair to face his superior's computer and began typing. "Here," he said a few seconds later, "I have it open."

"Can you search for 'Milton Wax'?" Daphna stepped toward the screen, forgetting everything else. She was suddenly in her element.

Dexter stepped away to give her room.

Brother Joe typed in the name. "Two hits," he said when the results came up.

"We visited twice," Daphna said, disappointed.

"How about 'Adem Tarik'?" Dex suggested.

"Nothing," Brother Joe said after entering the name.

"He probably used a fake name," Daphna sighed. "I mean another fake name. We'll never—Could it have been Mom? Try Latona Pellonia." When that search also came up empty she suggested Shimona Wax, and then finally Sophia Logos, her mother's original name.

No hits.

"I don't get it," Daphna complained. "Neither of them brought it here. Neither of us did, obviously. Hold on, can you look up 'Evelyn Idun'?" She figured they might as well try everything.

Brother Joe keyed in the name.

A hit.

Daphna leaned into the screen, nearly shoving the monk aside. "She was here!" she cried jabbing the screen with her finger. "Last year! Wait a minute!" she added, straightening up to look at her brother. "She came the day after she moved in with us last summer! It's her book, Dex! Why didn't she tell us? She had plenty of time to tell us!"

"You *saw* it," Dex moaned, upset that his normally pre-cise memory had let him down. Of course, it was actually his sister's memory. "You saw it in the back of that cabinet in the Records Room at the Home," he explained. "A huge book with straps built into the cover you said. But then we got dis-tracted."

"You're right!" Daphna realized. "I forgot all about it! Maybe she thought she didn't need it after—after Dad was gone." She turned to Brother Joe. "Where was it, anyway?"

"In a safe for dangerous books," the monk explained. "It could have remained there for a hundred years. Longer. Who exactly are you two?"

"I'll bet she hid it here because she couldn't destroy it," Dex said.

"What do you know about this book?" Brother Joe asked. "I'm quite sure it had something to do with what—came, and now I'm quite certain the abbot was seeking this Evelyn Idun, if the book was indeed hers, for help. I've been searching his study for anything that might allow me to be of service, but I've found nothing."

That explained the state of the office, the twins both real-ized. But they hesitated to share what they knew.

"There are rumors about Abbot Augustine," Brother Joe said.

"Rumors?" the twins asked back.

"The abbot is—he *was*—famous for his interim leadership abilities. He took over abbeys in crisis. His job was to stabilize them and move on. Otherwise, he traveled the world offering advice to various Church organizations. But there has long been talk that he was much more than an advisor."

"What do people think he was?" Daphna asked.

"The most popular theory is that he was an exorcist."

"An exorcist?" Dex and Daphna both yelped.

"Any other theories?" Daphna asked, hoping for some-thing less unnerving.

"Yes," said Brother Joe, "that he was a demon hunter."

That sounded worse.

"What—what do you think?" Dex asked.

Brother Joe looked around at the maps on the study's walls. "I think the abbot was looking for the book Evelyn Idun brought here," he said. "I think whatever has been attacking people in libraries around the world has been too. And I think it came here. I can't speculate any further until I know exactly what that book is. If only I'd been able to examine it."

Daphna decided to take a risk. She pulled the book out of her bag and set it on the abbot's desk. Dex was surprised, but didn't protest. "I'm sorry we didn't tell you we had it," she said. "But we have to be careful about who we trust."

Seeing the book was clearly the last thing Brother Joe expected. He put his hand on the cover, then touched the symbol with his finger.

"What is that?" Daphna asked. "I mean inside the compass rose."

"An aleph," Brother Joe said. "It's the first letter of the Hebrew alphabet."

The twins eyed each other. Hebrew again. It was Hebrew that helped them figure out the Garden of Eden was a library. They were both sure this symbol was important.

"It's full of maps," Dexter said. "Um, very unusual maps. Take a look."

"As you can probably tell, Abbot Augustine was obsessed with maps," Brother Joe explained as he opened the book. "That is the main reason a small minority believed he was actually searching for—" The monk's mouth opened, but no more words came out. After a few moments, he began to turn the impossibly thin pages.

"Incredible, isn't it?" Daphna said.

*"The Kingdom,"* Brother Joe whispered, his voice distant and small. *"The Empire.* The Universe!" He was gingerly touching a declivity in a map, nearly stupefied to see his finger dip into the page.

"Do you know what it is?" Dex asked.

"A map," the stunned monk recited, "whose size was that of the empire, coinciding point for point with it." He seemed to be talking to himself. Then he looked at the twins directly and said, "It's a map of all God's creation. A boundless book with infinite pages, as infinite as the universe itself."

Before the twins could react to this, Brother Joe leapt to his feet. "It's—it's *real!*" he cried, taking a large step away from the book. "It's cursed! It's true about Augustine! The Black Death!"

"What?" the twins cried. It was shocking to see Brother Joe's expression fly from fascination to fear so quickly.

The now-horrified monk kept backing away from the desk, wringing his hands. *"That book,"* he gasped, "has been associated with death and disease throughout history. It is said to have caused plagues! Diseases that came on black winds!"

Dexter and Daphna looked at each other yet again. Both had gone ashen. Did Evelyn have the Plague? Did they? But they couldn't. Surely they'd be sick already if that was the case, given how quickly Evelyn got ill. Daphna pulled the abbot's phone out of her bag and began tapping it.

"I don't think it's the book that makes people sick," Dex said. "I think it's okay."

"Why do you say that?" Brother Joe demanded. He'd been watching Daphna work the phone, but now he honed in on Dex as if the answer meant life or death to him. Perhaps it did. He'd touched the book.

"I think there's more to the story," Dex replied. "I don't think the disease comes on the wind—exactly. You said something came here. I hurt it. I might even have actually kill—"

"Oh, no!" Daphna cried. She'd found what she'd been searching for on the Internet. "The Black Plague!" she read. "Swollen lymph nodes and dark patches on the skin! Most victims died *within four to seven days after infection!* Dexter!"

"The abbot was searching for that book," Brother Joe said, taking a seat in a chair by the door, "probably for sixty years." The young monk's blue eyes moved about the room, unfocused. He was thinking hard and fast, rubbing the stubble on his chin.

Dex decided not to process Daphna's latest news. That way it just couldn't be true.

"How could the abbot have known it would be at an abbey?" Daphna wondered aloud. She was trying to forget what she'd just learned as well. "They aren't the only places with old, religious books."

"That would have been his area of expertise," Brother Joe explained as a glimmer of comprehension bloomed in his eyes. "There would be others, a larger group—My God!" he exclaimed, back on his feet. "Augustine was a member of the Cartographers Guild!"

"The what?" asked the twins.

Brother Joe could barely contain his excitement. "There's a story everyone with a religious vocation hears some time in his life," he said. "But that's all anyone ever takes it for—a story!"

"What is it?" the twins urged.

"A group of high priests from many ancient cultures were said to have collaborated to make this book. Others say they did not create it but rather formed around its discovery to plumb its mysteries and to protect it. Either way, the Guild is said to have lost the Book in the chaos after Babel. According to the legend, each generation of new members has been searching for it since. Centuries! And they are deadly! Whenever the Book is rumored to have resurfaced, they are said to gather—"

At that moment the sound of cars, many cars, drew everyone's attention to the abbot's large window. The twins and Brother Joe rushed to it.

A long line of vehicles was winding into the lot.

# CHAPTER SEVEN
### The Cartographers Guild

The first car, a sport utility vehicle with tinted windows, pulled into a spot and stopped. A man emerged from the back seat wearing a slate gray suit and tie—and a hippopotamus mask. A second door opened and a woman in a long, black dress emerged. She was also wearing a mask: a crocodile. Dozens of cars were settling into spaces around them.

"They've come *here!*" Brother Joe cried. Then he seemed to leave himself again, lost in thought, staring at the increasingly crowded parking lot. Dozens of people in masks—all hippos and crocodiles—were emerging from cars. One of them pointed toward the library.

"You must go," Brother Joe said, snapping out of his daze. He looked both Dexter and Daphna in the eyes. "I will stay and learn what they want with the book," he said. "Let me lock it up. I can call you when it's safe to come back. Here, let me get the abbot's number from the phone."

Daphna handed Brother Joe the phone, but said, "We can't give you the book. And we're going to stay."

Brother Joe looked quickly out the window. The masked arrivals were all inspecting robes on the ground. But one was urging them to move on. "We don't have time!" Brother Joe warned. "Your lives are in danger!"

"We don't have a choice," Dexter explained. "Someone is very sick, and we need to find out how to help her."

"How can we all hide here?" Brother Joe asked, looking wildly around the office.

"Don't worry," Daphna promised, eyeing the library through the office door. "We'll figure something out."

Brother Joe looked torn, but gave in to the twins' resolve. He made a slight bow and said, "God be with you." He tapped on the phone a few times, looking for its number, then handed it back. "If something goes wrong, I'll call," he promised. Then he climbed under the abbot's desk.

"There!" Dex said, pointing into the library. Brother Joe had given him an idea. He turned off the light and stepped outside. Daphna, after shoving the book and phone back into her bag and closing the door, followed her brother, who was darting to the library's main desk. The entry doors were pushed open just as the pair threw themselves underneath. There was barely enough room, so they found themselves crammed together, close enough not to be sure whose heart was pounding on whose ribs.

*Here we go again,* Dexter thought.

From the sounds of it, the room was quickly filling up. "Secure the building!" someone ordered. Immediately thereafter came the sounds of purposeful movement. Doors opening all around.

*"Brother Joe!"* Daphna whispered. She'd managed to contort herself in such a way that she could see out into the library from under the bottom edge of the desk, where it didn't quite meet the floor. Dex was squashed nearly flat in the process, but she had to see. Someone was opening the abbot's office—only there was so much noise and commotion all around, and passing legs kept blocking her line of sight. It was impossible to know what was happening in there. Of course, it would probably become obvious if Brother Joe was discovered.

The door stayed open for what seemed an awfully long time, but then, finally, she saw black dress shoes come out. Daphna sighed when the door was closed and managed to return to her previous, only slightly less uncomfortable position. Dex managed to breathe again.

"Clear!" someone called, and the bustle in the room dwindled quickly. People found seats.

When it got quiet, a stately baritone voice addressed the group. "Greetings Members of the Guild!" it proclaimed. "As your hierarch, I welcome you all, and I congratulate those who have traveled great distances on such short notice. But you will forgive me for getting right down to business. There will be, of course, no introductions."

"To business!" a voice with a foreign accent concurred. Australian maybe. Several others echoed the approval with other accents—other languages as well, it seemed.

"We have all received the message from Abbot Augustine," the hierarch continued, "but by now you all surely know something has gone wrong since he found the Book."

"The Black Wind!" someone cried. "Is it true?"

"You saw the robes!" someone else called out. "Is same in these attacks, no?"

This set off a volley of murmurs and shouts. The twins could feel both disbelief and fear sweep through the library like toxic fumes.

One voice boomed above the others. "The curse is real!" it declared. "But what came here was worse than any plague!"

"It was *here!*" someone else wailed. "The demon was here!"

This led to an explosion of wild exclamations.

Dex and Daphna, unable to see each other's eyes, had both gone rigid. *A demon?*

The commotion intensified. Shouts of "Ridiculous!" and "Absurd" rang out.

The hierarch called for quiet, which he eventually got. "There is little doubt that we face a grave and gathering threat," he told the anxious crowd, "from whatever the source. Does this not but highlight the urgency of our quest?"

This proved persuasive enough. The crowd settled down with diminished, but still audible muttering.

"I've heard rumors about Augustine!" a woman called out. Scottish? "That he was also looking for some kind of charms."

"Fairy tales!" a skeptic bellowed. "Wishful thinking! There is no protection but faith!"

*"That thing you stabbed it with,"* Daphna whispered. *"There must be more."* Dex felt his hand throb simply by having to think about it again. It still hurt a lot.

"It seems that Abbot Augustine believed the talismans were real," the hierarch acknowledged. "But I do not believe he ever learned exactly what they are or how they function."

"But are they real?" someone demanded.

"Does he have one?"

"Let us hope they are, and let us hope he does," the hierarch said. "But," he urged, "we must focus on the Book. We must determine our course of action swiftly. It has been centuries since we have come so close. Let us not allow our fears to deter us."

Grudging consent was voiced around the library.

The twins finally dared to relax, slightly. At least no one knew they were there.

"What do we do?" someone asked. "Is Augustine alive? Where is he?"

"Call him!" someone suggested. The voice was very hoarse.

Daphna lunged for her bag—the abbot's phone was in there!—slamming her head into Dexter's in the process. He struggled to give her room as his vision filled with flashing sparks.

"It's no use, friend," the hierarch said. "We have tried repeatedly." But then he added, "Perhaps one last time."

The twins were making a racket under the desk, but it didn't matter. Daphna had to get that phone turned off. She managed to find and dump her bag. *Why didn't she silence it when she had the chance?* She snatched it off the floor and managed to get the screen lit up, but it was too late.

Church bells chimed under the desk.

Dead silence fell over the library.

Daphna slid the phone as hard as she could out from under the desk. It kept ringing as it skidded away.

A great rustle sounded as everyone in the room stood up. Then the very air went still as every ear bent to discern the direction from which the bells chimed.

"Here!" someone cried. The bells stopped.

Daphna closed her eyes. *Please let them think he lost it there.*

The next minute felt like forever.

Dexter held his breath, but he hadn't closed his eyes, so he saw the eyes that appeared below the desk, blinking at him from behind a hippopotamus mask.

# CHAPTER EIGHT
## Shows

The hippo who'd discovered the twins was a small man in a business suit plainly too big for him. He shouted for help, and from his hoarse voice, the twins could tell that he'd also been the one who'd suggested calling the abbot. Two beefy crocodiles rushed over, grabbed Dexter by the bandaged hand, and yanked him, yowling, out of the hiding spot.

Daphna grabbed her bag and came out directly behind him, shouting in an effort to distract anyone and everyone from noticing that the Book of Maps had fallen out with the phone and was lying on the floor. Fortunately, no one thought to check under the desk after searching her bag.

The twins were forced into two chairs there. The hippos and crocodiles, all elegantly dressed in international styles, crowded around them. If the group wasn't exuding such malice, the twins could acknowledge how absurd everyone looked. But the silly looking lot wasn't, they both knew, planning to entertain them.

Dexter steeled himself. There was no need to panic yet. They'd been through worse. Daphna closed her eyes and told herself she would not go to pieces. It was going to be okay.

"Ah," Dex said, when he'd recovered enough saliva to speak, "is there some kind of show going on?"

"Yeah," Daphna added, opening her eyes. "We didn't mean to spy on your rehearsal. We thought we'd get in trouble if you knew we—"

A tall, but slightly stooped crocodile wearing a long, silver cassock of some sort over white sneakers, waved aside her words. When he spoke, the gravity of the voice told the twins he was the leader, the hierarch. "Paradise Books," was the first thing he said. "What is that?"

It took a moment for the twins to realize he was talking about their shirts.

"It's—nothing," Daphna said. "A store. They were giving away shirts for a promotion. We like to read."

"Why did you have the abbot's phone?" the hierarch demanded. His eyes flashed bright green under his mask.

"We didn't mean to steal it," Dex replied. "We found it out in the parking lot and thought it was really neat."

"Where do you live?"

This surprised the twins. They didn't know whether the truth was advisable. "Around here," Dex said.

"I see. And how did you get here today?"

"Ah—I drove," Dex said.

"He's sixteen," Daphna explained. It was impossible to tell how any of this was going over because the masks were obviously not registering any expressions. They looked somehow both silly and severe. A female crocodile in a multicolored skirt was taping the abbot's phone, and it was driving them both to distraction.

"You'll have keys then," said the hierarch.

Dex was happy to prove this. He made an effort to fish them out, but it wasn't easy because there were a bunch of them on the ring and he had to reach into his right pocket with his left hand. But he managed and handed them over.

The hierarch held them up. A large cross jangled among the bunch.

"Very religious then, are we?"

"Very," said Daphna. "That's why we feel so—"

"Can you read this for me?" The hierarch was holding another attachment to the ring, a metal plate of some kind. The twins' hearts skipped a beat. Was it another talisman? He held it out to Dexter, but Daphna took it.

"Return to Mt. Angel Abbey," she read, and her heart sank.

"A ha!" said the crocodile in the skirt, handing the phone to her leader. "They came from Portland."

"In the abbot's car, I'm guessing," the hierarch said after glancing at the screen. "It appears that the only performance here, children, is yours."

"Where is Augustine?" someone demanded. "What have you done with him?"

"Make them speak!" came a harsh demand from somewhere else. Many other hippos and crocodiles echoed the call. Daphna was quickly becoming less certain about keeping it together. The exit wasn't far, but it lay beyond too many bodies.

"He found it!" someone shouted. "There!"

This silenced the room. It was a hippo wearing a turban, pointing at the hippo in the oversized suit, who'd apparently decided to look under the desk after all. He was holding the

Book of Maps.

"No!" Daphna cried as the crowd surged to get a look. "If you touch it," she warned, "the Black Wind will come! The—the *demon* will wither you away!"

Now the herd backed away from the little hippo, who remained were he stood, holding the fearsome book. He didn't seem to know what to do with it now.

The room caught its breath. Masks tipped up as anxious eyes probed the sky through the curving windows overhead. Even the twins felt their eyes pulled upward.

No one moved a muscle for what felt like ages.

Finally, someone cried out. "It's not true! It's not true! We are safe!"

"Thanks to God!" someone shouted, and the call was echoed around the library. One by one, the animals lowered their gazes and turned their attention back to the book.

The hierarch set down the phone and held out his hand. The little hippo hesitated—perhaps not wishing to endanger his leader—but then handed it over.

The anticipation in the library was enormous as the hierarch considered the prize. For a moment, he inspected the symbol on the cover, but then looked inside. He nodded slightly at what he saw, then immediately raised the open book over his head for the crowd, which gasped at the sight of the moving maps inside.

"The Book of Maps!" cried the hierarch of the Cartographers' Guild. "Our treasure! Our key! It is ours again at last!"

A roar went up. Minor chaos ensued as the entire group pushed forward to get a closer look.

No one saw Daphna stuff the phone into her pocket. It might have been the cause of their present troubles, but she figured they ought to have a way to call for help if they absolutely had to.

"I must study it immediately!" a crocodile declared. He sounded Indian. It seemed everyone was declaring much the same in too many languages to count.

The hierarch seemed too fascinated by what he held in his hands to deal with the unruliness. But finally he called for order, and eventually everyone took seats again. The atmosphere in the room had transformed entirely. The twins looked at each other and wordlessly proposed making a break for it, but they'd missed their opportunity. The beefy crocodiles kept them where they sat with four heavy hands on their shoulders. At least they were no longer the center of murderous attention.

"We must," the hierarch declared, "determine the most efficient way to study the Book. It will, no doubt, require our collective expertise to interpret the maps. This is the opportunity of a lifetime, of many, many lifetimes."

"I can do it myself!" someone insisted. A Frenchman.

"Go back to your tower!" someone snapped at him.

"I maintain that Eiffel is a gate!" he snapped back.

This brought down a barrage of guffaws.

"Order!" the hierarch demanded.

"Perhaps modern technology is the solution!" came a call—the little hippo once again. His voice sounded very strained. It was hard to hear.

"What do you propose?" the hierarch asked.

"Word of the crisis here has not reached the outside world," the hippo explained. "I suggest we remain here. We will close the abbey for an extended retreat. There," he added, pointing to an odd-looking lamp on the main desk with two heads on flexible arms. It had a cord running to the desktop computer.

*"It's a document camera,"* Daphna whispered.

The hierarch didn't seem to know what it was, but he handed the book over. The little hippo set it open under the camera and turned the power on. Then he pulled down a screen mounted on the wall behind the desk. As soon as it was lowered, a map appeared. Little sparkles appeared here and there once again.

Gasps erupted again, all around.

"I see!" an elated voice blurted, breaking the spell. "I see!"

"The gates!" someone else proclaimed. People seemed to be pointing to the pinpricks of light.

Once again everyone was on their feet. No one was going to tolerate a blocked view, so a pushing match broke out as the hippos and crocodiles struggled for an unobstructed view. Even the beefy crocodiles let go of the twins' shoulders and moved in for a look.

*Now* was the time.

Daphna and Dexter got up and, with heads down, walked swiftly toward the door. They passed directly through the fringe of the jockeying crowd, ready to run if they had to. But no one noticed them. Dex got to the door first and tore it open. Then he and Daphna threw themselves outside—into two brutish hippos wearing ear buds. The guards grabbed the twins by the arms and twisted them behind their backs.

The crowd was still jostling at the screen when Daphna

and Dex were a hauled back inside. Someone saw them and started hollering for attention. Slowly, others took notice.

The room went quiet. All masks turned to the captives.

"We must deal with this—distraction," the hierarch told the crowd. "These children," he added, "will tell us what they know of Abbot Augustine, or they will die."

The twins, both hunched over in attempt to relieve the pain in their arms, had been expecting to hear something like this, but that made it no less unpleasant. Memories of all they'd gone through came flooding back for both of them. Dexter knew the time to use his switchblade was now, but his good arm was being broken and his bad hand couldn't manage the job.

"We're not telling you anything!" he spat. "You'll kill us anyway!"

"Kill them!" someone suggested. "We have the Book! Be done with it! Quickly!"

The hierarch nodded.

The hippo wrenching his arm let go, so Dex ripped the switchblade out of his pocket. It was open in a flash. He brandished it at the hippo who'd turned him loose, but the man was suddenly not even looking at him. He had a finger on his earbud and was looking up at the windows above. Both of the hippo guards were.

"He's got a knife!" someone cried from the crowd, which brought forth demands to disarm Dexter. The crowd had circled round, but no one dared approach.

Dex didn't know what to do. He spun around, brandishing the blade at anyone and everyone. Daphna, feeling faint, jammed herself up against him.

There was a lull in the shouting, and one of the guards spoke into it. "Dexter and Daphna Wax?"

The twins, baffled, nodded.

"What's going on!" someone demanded.

Now the guards were backing away. The one who'd said their names looked at the hierarch and said, "The CDC is searching for these kids. They may have been exposed to a new strain of the Plague!"

This was the last straw for the members of the Cartographer's Guild. The room was instantly engulfed in plain and simple panic. Hippos and crocodiles scrambled willy-nilly to get as far away from the twins as possible.

Dex and Daphna were stunned by the sudden turn of events and couldn't decide what to do.

"Run!" Daphna finally cried. But before the twins could

break for the exit again, a noise—a massive noise, like a train—bore down from overhead. Everyone in the room stopped dead and once again looked up to the overhead windows.

A helicopter, huge and blue, was descending on the library.

Then came sounds that drew all eyes to the front windows. A line of white vans and trucks were screaming into the parking lot. Each was labeled with three large letters: CDC.

"*Dios Mio!*" someone cried. "We will die!"

Everyone was too stunned to react now. Or no one knew what to do. Figures in blue hazardous materials suits were suddenly sprinting around the perimeter of the library, some unwinding yellow tape as they went.

The twins saw the red scarves on their arms right away.

"The Book!" shouted the hierarch. "Get—!"

But before he could complete his instruction, something broke through one of the overhead windows and landed on the floor amidst a burst of broken glass, a canister of some kind, and it started spraying gas. Now windows were breaking all around. Many canisters hit the floor, spinning and spraying every which way.

Pandemonium ensued.

Like a spooked herd, the Cartographer's Guild ran in all directions, flinging their masks off to breathe. It was quickly discovered that the doors were barred, and this sent the group into wild paroxysms of despair. Strangely, despite their own desperation, both twins shared the same thought about the unmasked guild: *It's just an ordinary group of people.*

But the gas, or smoke, whatever it was, was filling up the room.

Brother and sister grabbed hands and ran, but inevitably, they were separated by bodies colliding in the bedlam. It seemed only seconds before they were calling each other's names.

Daphna fumbled around looking for Dex until something tripped her. She fell hard, but it was easier to breathe on the floor. She crawled blindly until she found a door, which she was able to push open. Her eyes were stinging, but she managed to see she was in the abbot's study. The room was filling with smoke. There was a body on the floor, which at first Daphna did not react to. But then she realized who it must be.

"Brother Joe!" she cried. How could she have forgotten him? Wheezing and on the verge of blacking out, Daphna dragged herself toward the body over the books and papers on the floor. Two bare feet protruded from behind the desk.

She managed to reach them, but collapsed, choking. The last thing she saw were a pair of sandals sitting on the carpet next to the legs, resting in a small puddle of blood.

Dex was also scrabbling on the floor, searching for breathable air. He could hardly open his eyes. The only thing he could do was feel around blindly for his sister. His injured hand protested the weight he put on it, and his throat was on fire. He could not call out.

Other bodies were on the floor. One crawled over him. It was just like the burning bookstore. How could he be in this position again? He heard a voice cry out, the hierarch's. Dex saw the silver cassock, then white sneakers as he fumbled past on all fours. Despite his panic, Dexter noticed that one sneaker had a much thicker heel than the other. The hierarch's legs were different lengths. He was defective too.

Dex rolled away and found himself looking at a door. It was open! He got to his feet and sprinted toward it, but he immediately crashed into someone, someone kneeling with his hands in the air, offering what had to be a prayer. Dex scrambled to his feet again, but after two steps crashed into furniture of some sort. Equipment fell to the floor. There were sparks. Something else fell and landed on his foot. He was losing consciousness, but he knew what it was. Dex crouched down and grabbed it.

He had the Book of Maps.

"I got it!" Dex howled. But then it was ripped from his hands.

And then his thoughts simply ceased.

# CHAPTER NINE
*The Joy of Popularity*

Daphna's body was vibrating, and her head felt like it was filled with cement. Some sort of awful grunting and scratching sound came from somewhere nearby. She forced open her burning, blurry eyes to see—nothing. It was dark. She tried to put a hand to her aching head, but her arm wouldn't move. Neither would. Nor would her legs.

The void that had swallowed her mother, the void that had swallowed her peace-of-mind every night—it had taken her now too. She was dead.

But she could think.

"Mom!" Daphna cried. "Are you here?"

"*Shh! Shut up!*" someone hissed. Was that Dexter?

Slowly, painfully, Daphna turned her head toward the voice. Was there a figure there, darker than the dark around it? There was another noise, she finally noticed, fairly loud, a humming, grinding sort of sound. An engine? Yes! And she was moving.

She was not dead. She was in a vehicle.

The grunting and scratching came again.

Then, a voice right over her face.

"Center for Disease Control—yeah, right," Dexter said. He was loosening whatever bound Daphna. She could move her legs. "They got the Book," he added, "which I suppose means they won't be offering us a billion dollars for it anymore."

Daphna was free, but couldn't sit up. And it took a few moments for Dexter's words to filter down through the swirling haze in her mind. They did sink in, but a coherent reply was more than she could manage for the moment.

"These scarf-wearing kidnappers probably saved our lives," Dexter said as his silhouette moved away. "I feel like complete and total crap."

In silence, Daphna stared up into the dark, trying to clear her head and to avoid feeling the disappointment of not see-ing her mother again. After what felt like half an hour, though it could have been just a few minutes, she began to feel like herself again.

Very carefully, as if she'd break things in her brain, Daphna sat up. "We're in one of those vans," she realized.

"Yep," her brother's voice replied in the dark.

"How long have we been driving?"

"No idea, but I know I'm starving to death again. I don't suppose there's any food in here. A little light would help."

"The phone!" The thrill of remembering she had it threatened to make Daphna's head explode, but she reached into her pocket and pulled it out. It was still on, and had a lot of power left. She held out its glowing screen.

They were indeed in a van. White, ribbed metal walls. They'd been strapped to stretchers, the kind that fold down over wheels to fit in ambulances.

"How'd you get free?" Daphna asked.

"Strap broke," Dex replied.

Daphna leaned over Dex's stretcher pointing the phone like a flashlight. She saw the strap, which had been roughly severed. *That scratching noise.* She aimed the phone at Dex to see him shrug.

"I guess it broke with this," he said, holding up the switchblade.

Daphna blinked at the knife. "Oh, nice one," she said.

Dex was pleased with his sister's non-reaction to his carrying a weapon, but she was obviously not thinking clearly. He'd come out of whatever fog that gas had put him into quite a while ago. When Daphna wouldn't respond to his whispers, he'd spent the time—too hard to tell how long it'd been—wrestling his knife free, working it open, and sawing like crazy. It made his hand feel like its skin was being torn off, but he fought through it, grateful to have shoved the knife into his front pocket at the abbey.

"Hey!" Daphna cried. "We can call for help!"

"Shhh! Call who? Those guys said the actual CDC is looking for us, which I guess we should be happy about since *they* saved our lives too. But if we call, we'll be quarantined."

"Well," Daphna replied, "you wanted us to turn ourselves in, didn't you? Doesn't quarantined sound better than killed?"

"But Evelyn is the one who's going to die, Daphna. You said she might not live more than a week!"

"Shhh!" Daphna warned back. "Okay," she conceded, "you're right. We'll call for help only as a last resort. Only we're not waiting so long next time. And we're not *stabbing* anybody."

That was more like her. "Fine," Dex said. "We won't stab

any *people.*"

"Right," Daphna agreed. There was no need to say more on that subject. Now that she could think, she remembered who else she'd forgotten. *"Brother Joe!"* she whispered.

"Did you see him?"

"I was in the office. He was on the floor, not moving. There was blood. His sandals were off."

"I'm sure he's okay," Dex said. "He probably took them off to sneak around better, and he probably passed out and hit his head from the gas. They weren't trying to kill anyone—other than us, I mean. I just wish we knew where we were going."

"I don't know, Dex," Daphna worried. "Hey, let's see where we are!" Daphna looked down at the phone. First she muted it like she should have on the way to the abbey. Then she opened the app and waited for their map to appear.

"We're heading into Central Oregon," Daphna said when it came up. "It's past one thirty. We've been driving for hours."

"That really is like the Book of Maps, isn't it?" Dex said, looking at the slowly shifting image marking their progress in the dark, not that it looked much clearer than the book to him.

"Sort of, yeah," Daphna agreed.

The light from the phone illuminated her face for a moment, and Dex saw she'd been badly shaken. He wondered what she'd been thinking when she cried out for their mother. Of course, she did that all the time at home in her sleep.

"What *is* that book, Dex?" Daphna asked. "Is it another one from the Library of Eden? Could it have a map *to* Eden in it? If it has the entire universe in it, it must, right? Is that why everyone's after it?"

"That would certainly be worth a billion dollars," said Dex. "But we never came across anything about a map to Eden when we—when *you*—were looking up all that stuff about it. With all those famous people searching for the Garden—someone would have mentioned a map."

"You helped," Daphna pointed out. "Hey, speaking of research, let's see what we can learn from the web."

"Okay."

"Let's start with the 'Book of Maps.'" Daphna typed the phrase into a search engine. "Nothing useful, of course," she said when the results came up. She found nothing useful with "Cartographer's Guild," either. "Oh, my gosh!"

"What?"

"He has a banner with news flashes." Daphna started

reading. "Possible case of Plague variant in Portland, Oregon. CDC on high alert. Two children sought in connection with first known case in modern—Hold on," she said, breaking off, "I'm tapping through."

A moment later, she was linked to a national news page. Her voice quavered as she read:

"An elderly woman residing in Portland, Oregon, Evelyn Idun, is thought to be presenting symptoms of the Black Plague, the deadly disease responsible for millions of deaths between the twelfth and fifteenth centuries. Local, state, and federal agencies are treating the case with utmost caution.

"The victim has been isolated at Oregon Health Sciences University and is under the care of world-renowned stem cell researcher and infectious disease expert, Dr. Roberta Fludd. Questions as to the specific variant of the disease and the mechanism by which it may spread have not been answered.

"There are three variants of the plague: Bubonic, characterized by swelling of the lymph nodes, is believed to be transmitted by fleas on rodents or bats; Pneumonic, which attacks the respiratory system, can be spread by simply breathing exhaled air from a victim; and Septicemic, which attacks the circulatory system.

"As a precaution, medical professionals are going house to house in Ms. Idun's neighborhood to administer vaccinations. The victim's two adopted teens, Daphna and Dexter Wax (pictured above), are missing and may be fleeing out of fear (see link here for the Wax twins in the news last year in connection with the murders of several members of a local old-age home managed by Ms. Idun). A statewide search is now underway. If any citizen sees either of the children, he or she is advised not to approach them, but rather to alert authorities at once. Click this link for the number.

"See sidebar for a description of symptoms associated with the various diseases often grouped under the name 'Plague.'"

Dexter!" Daphna cried, "Our pictures are here! I look terrible. DEX!"

Dex had been appalled while he listened to his sister read, but also absurdly pleased to find himself on the national news, to be at the center of a crisis big enough to warrant the attention of—well, given the reach of the web—probably the whole world. It was the same feeling he'd had seeing his face on television last year, but even stronger. After everything they'd done, the world should know who they were. But that was stupid. "We can't go home," he realized.

The last safe place was gone.

This hit Daphna hard. Tears welled up again, but she stifled them. She was sick of crying. "The government is looking for us," she moaned, "those Cartographer people are probably looking for us, and we don't even know who has us right now!"

"Nice to be popular," Dex said.

Daphna actually laughed at this. "My dream come true at last," she said, darkly. "Anyway, we need to figure out what they were doing at that meeting. What did they say? It was impossible to understand half of it with everyone babbling in fifty different—"

"Wait!" Dex said. "Brother Joe said *Babel*. He said the Cartographer's Guild lost the Book after Babel. Maybe he meant the Tower of Babel. And we better keep our voices down."

*"Right!"* Daphna whispered. "I've read about that! People were trying to build a tower to reach God at Babel. I think that's the story anyway. Hold on, I'm looking it up."

"Why does everyone looking for God seem willing to kill people along the way?"

"True," Daphna said, but with only half her attention. She'd found an entry and was skimming it. "I was right," she said. "The Tower was built by a united humanity to reach God."

"So Dad was trying to get God to come to him, and the Guild was trying to get to God. Same difference, really. Oh, yeah—didn't God scramble everyone's languages so they couldn't keep working? Hey, just like the pages of the Book of Nonsense."

"Yeah," Daphna agreed. "But I thought the tower was destroyed too. I thought it collapsed. I don't see anything about that here."

"But God couldn't really have messed up people's languages and destroyed the tower, right? That would be interfering with free will. He was gone long before then, whenever it was."

"Maybe he made an exception," Daphna said. "Hold on. Here's something about the collapse of the tower." She read a moment, then said, "It says there's nothing about the destruction in the Bible, but there is in other books. They say the tower was overturned in a great—Oh!" Daphna caught herself up short.

"What?" Dex asked. But then he knew. "Don't tell me," he said. "*Wind.*"

Daphna nodded. The dim light from the phone revealed

the fear in her face, made all the more ominous by the rumbling of the van. "God didn't destroy it," she said. "*She* did. Dex, those people—the Guild—they said she was a demon. Did you stab a demon?"

"Maybe they're wrong," Dex replied, trying not to recall his certainty that he hadn't killed it. "Maybe I did kill it," he offered, deciding to be hopeful. The enormity of the possibility struck him hard. Could he, Dexter Wax, have killed a demon? If he had, people were going to know this time. He'd make sure of it. "I guess it would make sense that a demon wouldn't want mankind to find God," he said.

The twins went silent a moment, thinking about how, once again, they were up to their necks in something far, far beyond them. Who were *they*? Two nobodies going nowhere in the dark.

Story of their lives.

"Where was it?" Dex finally asked, trying to focus on details that wouldn't reduce them to quivering masses. "The Tower of Babel, I mean."

Again, Daphna surfed around on-line, happy to change the subject. A few minutes later she said, "You won't be surprised to learn that—"

"Different people say different things."

"Exactly. But it looks like most say Babylon, and that the tower might have been—hold on—a great *ziggurat* that fell to ruin there. Those are—"

"Pyramid-type things, I know," Dex said.

As careful as Daphna had become about not insulting his intelligence, she still often forgot that he remembered pretty much everything he heard. Though of course how was she supposed to know what he'd heard and what he'd skipped hearing.

"Maybe that's what all the pyramids were," Dexter wondered aloud, "attempts to reach God. Maybe only for the dead dude buried at the bottom, but still."

"That could be exactly it!" Daphna cried, stunned. "We studied the pyramids in sixth grade, remember? No one really knows what they were actually for—there were also those kind built by the Incas and Aztecs. Wait a minute! Weren't they wiped out by disease?"

Dex didn't know, but he was sure his sister was right. "So how do people decide where to build?" he asked. "Can you do it anywhere? Didn't that guy call the Eiffel Tower a gate?"

The question hung between the twins for a moment. Then they understood the obvious.

"That book!" Daphna cried. "Those maps! They mark the gates of Heaven!"

# CHAPTER TEN
## *The "CDC"*

The twins sat silent and still, taking this in.

"Heaven," Daphna said, wondering at the very word. "So they *are* looking for God."

"Or dead people," Dex joked, though it didn't come out as funny at all.

Daphna gasped at the thought, but the sound was lost as the van slowed down and merged onto a much bumpier road.

"Quick!" Dex said. "Where are we?"

Daphna checked the phone. "Somewhere called Condon," she said. "It's near Sunriver, I think."

"Isn't that some sort of fancy resort town?"

"Sunriver? Yeah. My friends—I mean lots of Pops have summer homes here. Obviously, I've never been."

Dexter let this pass. He was amazed to think that just a year ago he'd have pounced all over that slip of the tongue. Daphna hadn't made one like that in a long time.

"Dex!" Daphna said, trying to focus after everything they'd just figured out. They'd been foolish not to think ahead. "What are we going to do when they see we're loose?"

"Does it matter?" Dex asked. "I guess they'll take my knife, though."

"Where'd you get it?"

"From our friendly neighborhood gangster last year."

"Antin! How could I not remember that? But Dex, you shouldn't carry something like that."

"Really?"

"Okay, but they *are* going to take it when they see you cut the strap. And then they'll find the phone, which is our only link to—anything."

The van was bouncing along now rather severely, apparently on some kind of back road.

"What if I cut the middle straps off completely?" Dex asked, urgency raising his voice. "We can latch ourselves back up and pretend we're still out of it. Maybe they won't remember there were three."

"But our arms would be free. They'll know it wasn't right."

"What else can we do?"

The point was moot because the van was slowing to a crawl. Gravel crunched loudly beneath the tires.

They stopped.

*"Get back on!"* Dex hissed.

Daphna recognized that tone in her brother's voice. He'd thought of something. She lay down quickly and let him refasten her straps. The van's front doors opened and closed. They heard voices. Dex jumped on his stretcher and latched the leg and shoulder straps.

*"What are you doing?"* Daphna whispered.

"Cutting our losses."

Daphna had no idea what this meant, and keys were being inserted in the back doors. And now they opened. Blinding light poured into the van around two men in hooded blue hazmat suits. Their dark eyes were visible through clear plastic shields, which covered gas masks.

"What's he doing?" one of them shouted. His voice echoed inside his mask.

Daphna squinted. Dex was twisted and hunched under his straps, struggling.

"He's got a knife!" one of the men shouted. And then they were both suddenly gone. Dex unlatched himself, but stayed on his stretcher.

A few seconds later, the men were back, both pointing guns with long black silencers on their ends.

Dex calmly closed the knife, tossed it on the floor, and put up his hands.

"Get out here!" both men yelled. Dex obeyed. One came inside, freed Daphna, and ordered her out as well.

The twins stood blinking in the harsh sun. They ached. Their stomachs rumbled. It was hot. Very hot. One of the men had the switchblade, and Dex was relieved to see they were content enough with their "discovery" not to think about searching them further. Daphna rubbed her eyes while they adjusted to the light.

"You didn't search them back at the abbey?" one of the blue men asked the other. "Durante will have your hide."

"Move," the second blue man told the twins, who walked in the direction he indicated, crunching on heaps of seeds.

*"No garlic,"* Daphna whispered, peeking under the hand shielding her eyes.

Dexter nodded, wondering what it meant.

The twins could see that they were on farmland surrounded by low, scorched mountains patched with swatches of green. The high desert terrain was harsh, but beautiful. They were walking toward some kind of lodge, a gorgeous, sprawling log-style structure surrounded on three sides by forest. A hotel or resort of some kind? Three enormous trucks supporting half a dozen slowly rotating satellite dishes sat in the parking lot. Beyond them, resting in a field that bordered the woods, was a helicopter. It said "Life Flight" on its side and had a rose painted on its tail.

"Mr. Durante?" one of the men asked, apparently to a transmitter inside his helmet. "Jay Conrad here. We're on our way in. Clean?" he asked a moment later. "Roger that."

The men stopped and released their masks, which hissed as they opened.

The man who'd spoken, Conrad, was pockmarked and sallow. He looked nervous. "Their blood's been cleared," he told his partner, who looked mightily relieved at the news.

The twins looked down at their arms and saw puncture marks. They'd had their blood drawn and tested? The thought was sickening, but then again, they'd just been told they didn't have the Plague.

"Durante?" Dexter suddenly asked, recognizing the name. "As in Virgil Durante? As in one of the richest men in the world?"

The men nodded and waved them forward.

"Wasn't there just some news about him?" Daphna asked Dexter as they walked. "Isn't he that depressed weirdo who buys up anything freakish in the world, like unicorn horns and werewolf hides?"

"Yeah," said Dex, catching what looked like a smirk pass between the men. "He recently opened one of his museums in Seattle."

"Right! That was it."

They'd reached the entrance to the lodge.

"Not a word about that knife," Conrad said under his breath as he hustled the twins inside.

It was a hunting lodge by the look of the antlers on the walls, but the place was clearly not being used to house outdoorsmen, and it was designed for vacationers judging from the lobby-like check-in counter. But it seemed the entire place had been taken over. All the main floor furniture had been pushed aside to make room for a command and control center. There were portable workstations all over, each with laptops running screens full of maps. Men dressed in jeans and blazers and wearing headsets clicked away at nearly all of them. Many were leaping up and down before returning to their keyboards, shouting instructions to one another like traders on the floor of the Stock Exchange. There were larger monitors set up here and there, also running maps.

The whole effect was disorienting, like coming upon NASA headquarters in full crisis mode in the middle of nowhere. The floors were covered an inch deep in poppy seeds, but no one seemed to find that the least bit odd.

The twins had time to take all this in because they'd been stopped by their captors, who were climbing out of their hazmat suits.

Dex nudged his sister and pointed. Several high-speed printers were spitting out paper continuously around the room. One was right next to them, so they leaned over it. Maps from the Book. Now Daphna pointed. The Book of Maps was there, in the center of the room, sitting inside a large transparent box on a steel stand. Inside, a nozzle was pointing down at it, evidently shooting jets of air because the pages were turning every few seconds as if by an invisible hand. Each time one turned, a camera under the lid of the box snapped a picture, and it was those images that were appearing on monitors all around the room.

A gigantic stone fireplace rose up over the entire operation. On the hearth, the twins finally noticed, stood two striking men. The first couldn't possibly have looked more out of place. He was easily the oldest person there, though his age might have been anywhere between fifty and eighty. He was wearing some sort of traditional garb: a cloth cap that rose straight up on his head like a white eraser, a flowing brown button up top, and clashing black and blue plaid pants that looked rather like pajamas. He had dark skin and Asian eyes, and he was playing some sort of primitive looking flute with a wide end, though whatever sound he was producing was lost in the cacophony of the lodge. Hanging from his neck on a colorful twine was an empty bottle with a cork on top.

Standing next to him was another man, built far too powerfully to look natural in the tailored suit he sported. The cowboy boots seemed more appropriate. His head, an anvil, sat atop a neck that looked every bit as stout as the exposed beams crisscrossing the ceiling above it. The face, square-jawed and steely, was well tanned but deeply sorrowful. Daphna had seen this face on TV and remembered now how startlingly sad it looked.

"Mr. Durante?" Conrad called out.

Durante turned and took in the twins with melancholy

eyes. He nodded, and suddenly a dozen men in combat fatigues stepped out from—wherever they were hiding. A line of them was also suddenly up above, standing along the railing on the upper floor, all pointing those strange guns down at the twins. *Nail* guns, they now saw. Or nail rifles was more like it.

Dex and Daphna were each grabbed and hauled off in separate directions.

This was the last thing they expected.

"Dex!" Daphna cried, reaching for him.

Guns or not, Dexter tried to fight, but when his punch landed on the body armor of the man dragging him away, it hurt so badly he knew he'd not be able throw another. After that he could barely think as he found himself manhandled up a set of stairs and into a room.

Daphna didn't struggle, but rather screamed her brother's name until she was forced into a room on the lower level. She was shoved inside so forcefully that she fell over a bed and onto the floor on the other side. She was dazed, but unhurt, so she scrambled the phone out of her pocket and slid with it under the bed.

Enough was enough.

But no sooner had she tapped the screen to life, someone grabbed her by the ankles and yanked her out. Her head hit the bed frame. The phone fell to the floor.

The man who'd shoved her into the room snatched it up—Conrad again. "Damn!" he spat, jabbing at it. Then he slammed it on the corner of a dresser, cracking the screen. Daphna watched him warily from the floor, rubbing her head.

"I called for help," she lied. "And I'll tell Mr. Durant. About the knife too."

Conrad looked her dead in the eye. He didn't speak, but rather seemed to be thinking.

Daphna stood up, holding the man's stare, hoping against hope he believed her and that meant something good. She knew desperate people could do desperate things, seeing she was one of them.

Finally, Conrad spoke. "I can get you out of here," he said.

# CHAPTER ELEVEN
*Split Decision*

"What do you mean?" Daphna asked. This was, of course, nearly the best possible thing she could have hoped to hear, but it had to be too good to be true.

"There!" Conrad said, pointing to the window and toward the helicopter. "I take off in fifteen minutes. When I leave the room," he instructed, "break the window with the lamp, then get into the closet. I'll come back and find you gone. I'll tell everyone I saw you running into the woods. When they start the search, we'll run to the chopper."

"What?" Daphna's mind was unspooling. "No," she said. "Absolutely not. Not without my brother."

"You have one minute to decide. Or I'll just have to find another way to shut you up."

Now Daphna was frantic. She couldn't possibly leave without Dex. She was the one who made them promise to stick together no matter what—but she was being given a chance to save them both! Regardless of what this man thought, she hadn't called anyone. If she got away, she could get help. Or maybe getting away was the same as getting herself killed, a sure way to shut her up. "What do they want with us?" she cried, mad with indecision.

"He won't hurt him," Conrad promised. "Durante doesn't like messes. He wants to know what you know. He's aware that you've been involved in all kinds of clandestine activities involving extremely valuable books." Daphna looked down at her T-shirt and decided to change it as soon as possible. "He knows who your father was. And your mother too. He knows about that bookstore that burned down. But what he doesn't know is what that book with all the maps has to do with people getting sick. I'm flying to the hospital to get the story on the lady you live with before she dies."

"I'll go," Daphna said. She was looking around the room for a way to bring her brother with her, but there was no way. Reluctantly, she picked up the lamp. It was heavy, a beige ceramic base topped by a rippled brown shade. As she approached the window, the cord nearly jerked it out of her sweating hands. She yanked it out of the wall.

After pocketing the pieces of broken phone, Conrad hurried out.

Daphna stood at the window, which was bolted closed, no doubt to prevent her escape. Almost everything in the room was bolted down. She looked out at the helicopter. How could they have a Life Flight chopper? Then again, if that crackpot could pay a billion dollars for a book, he could have anything he wanted.

*Except us,* Daphna thought bitterly, and she hurled the lamp.

It went straight through the window and shattered on the ground below. Daphna turned fearfully to the door, but no one came through it. There wasn't quite enough room for someone to climb through the jagged shards remaining in the frame, so she pushed some out with her foot. She didn't get them all, but it would have to do.

Then Daphna rushed into the closet, closed it, and sat down. She was sweating into her hair, which she had to wipe off her face. The door had closely spaced slats tilting downward, so she could see a bit into the room if she stood back up. Someone came back in as she got to her feet. It was Conrad in a flight suit, holding a helmet. He approached the window, pushed a few more pieces of glass out, then turned and hurried back out of the room.

The heat from outside seeped into the closet as Daphna stood with arms wrapped tight around her chest, trying to keep it together. What if this didn't work?

Suddenly there was a rush of bodies into the room. They went directly to the window.

"There!" Conrad said. "She went into the woods. Someone didn't bolt the lamp down!"

"Yes I did, Mr. Durante!" another man cried. "I swear I did!" He sounded terrified.

"Shut up!" someone yelled—Durante, she assumed. His anger was frightening. "Get some people out there," he ordered. "Now!"

Everyone jumped to do his bidding, everyone but one.

"Shall I delay the flight to OHSU, sir? I could take her up and look for the girl."

"No, get going. She won't get far. I need to know what the medical team is really saying."

"Yes, sir."

Durante left, and Daphna heard a tremendous sigh. A few moments later, the closet door opened.

"Let's go." Conrad took Daphna by the arm and led her to the window. Outside, a dozen of Durante's flunkies headed into the woods. No one was looking back. After knocking more glass out of the frame with his boot, Conrad faced Daphna and showed her what was inside his helmet: a gun.

"You'll run ahead of me," he ordered. "If you fail to go directly to the helicopter, I will shoot you. No one will hear," he added, assuming correctly that she knew what a silencer was.

Daphna didn't bat an eye at the threat, real as she knew it was. She nodded.

Conrad looked at her severely for a moment, no doubt judging her capacity for doing what she was told. He didn't look entirely satisfied, but he climbed out through the window after pulling loose a last shard and tossing it outside. The ground was only a few feet below. Tentatively, Daphna put a leg through after him, but as soon as he could, Conrad grabbed it and helped her down.

"Go!" he hissed. And she did.

The gravel around the lodge immediately gave way to brown grass. The hot air seemed to scorch her lungs as Daphna ran, nearly hyperventilating. The helicopter was farther away than it appeared. As her feet pounded the hard packed field, she dared to glance toward the woods. Some of the men were visible among the trees, but only their backs. Daphna heard Conrad behind her. She assumed the gun was pointed at *her* back.

It was getting closer. A hundred yards maybe. Fifty or sixty now. Daphna pushed herself on.

Almost there.

Daphna looked up at the propellers atop the helicopter as she crossed their shadows. At that moment, her toe caught a bump in the ground, sending her off her feet. She tried to break the fall, but her wrists gave way. The moment her forehead hit the ground, she blacked out.

But Daphna was conscious a second later, though barely. She couldn't move, couldn't see, couldn't think. She was being picked up, but had no strength even to help. A metal door slid open. Then Daphna felt metal on her face as she was laid inside and shoved forward like a bag of sand. Her brain felt too large for her skull. Funny colors spun in her eyes.

The door slammed, and moments later the propellers began to spin. The noise was deafening. Daphna tried to roll over, but she couldn't. Suddenly, she was overcome with remorse. She couldn't do this. She couldn't leave her brother behind, no matter what. What had she been thinking? Somehow, she sat up. "Stop!" she tried to scream, but all that came out of her mouth was puke.

It didn't matter anyway. They were in the air.

*     *     *

Like his sister, Dex was shoved inside the room so hard, he fell over the bed and hit the floor on the other side. He broke his fall with his bad hand, which sent blinding flashes of stabbing pain through his brain again. Still, he got to his feet and tried to grab the lamp to use as a weapon, but it was bolted to the bedside table.

"Save it, tough guy," said the goon who'd pushed him. "Take a seat."

Dex glanced around the room as his vision cleared, looking for a means of escape. He was in a hotel room: bed, dresser, closet, window—which was also bolted. It was obvious he'd lose a fistfight, so he sat on the bed. He might as well try to figure out what was going on.

"You got the book," Dexter snapped. "What do you need us for? We don't even know what it is."

"Don't you?" someone replied. Durante. He was in the doorway, *filling* the doorway. "I wonder," he added. His voice was flat, monotone, totally bored.

"Well, don't," Dex insisted, trying to sound defiant. But he couldn't help swallowing nervously, which made his voice hitch. "Some monk guy brought it into our store."

"Then what happened?"

Dex didn't answer for a moment. Finally, he said, "You don't want to know. You wouldn't believe it anyway."

"Try me," Durante said. "I have a very open mind."

Dex remembered the man's hobbies, but he wasn't going to tell him anything.

"You saw the book's owner, didn't you?"

Dex looked Durante in the heavy lidded eye and said, "No."

"Let's go see his sister, shall we?" Durante said to his man. "I think she might be more cooperative. Didn't strike me as much of a fighter."

"Wait!" Dex said. "I do know something!" He wasn't going to be the reason they hurt Daphna. "Those people at the abbey," he said, "in the masks—they're called the Cartographer's Guild. They think the book shows how to find—" Dex hesitated.

Durante raised a brow, thick as a brush.

"Heaven."

"Yes," the huge man said, not the least bit surprised. He rubbed his football player-sized neck for a moment. "Single minded, those folks, but also prodigiously naïve. Not to mention laughably incompetent when it comes to securing their lines of communication. I wonder," he added, "do they want to move in with God? Or just pop in, perfect themselves, and come back?"

"What—what do you mean perfect themselves?"

"A silly but ancient belief about that chimera some call Heaven," Durante explained. His eyes were barely open, as if staying awake was a terrible strain. "If one was to enter, he'd become as the angels are: perfect. You seem rather taken with the idea," the giant of a man remarked, noting Dex's wide-eyes. "But there are many theories about what effects entering Heaven would have on a living man. Some say all divisions would fall away, between the self and others, between the living and dead—the whole duality mindset. That type of thing. Hokum, every bit of it."

Dex heard little of this, but managed to pull himself back from the far distant place his mind had flown to respond. "So you don't think it's about Heaven?" he asked.

"Those fools certainly think it is, but that's because those fools at Babel thought it was. But that tower was not destroyed for what it was reaching. It was destroyed for what it contained—the Book of Maps. And what destroyed it, I assure you, was no god."

"They think it's cursed," Dex said. "They think a demon wants it."

"Well, now," Durante said. "I'm a negotiator at heart. Perhaps an exchange of information is in order."

Dex nodded. He'd lie.

"What that book is for," Durante said, "remains to be seen. As for this 'demon,' the term has been applied to many creatures for many reasons, real and imagined. It might as well serve here as well. Regardless, the book belongs to a Pontianak, likely *the* Pontianak, and I will have it for my collection—dead or alive." Durante's voice was still flat, but also now sharp as a blade. "If I wind up with an angel or two pinned to a display board as well, so much the better."

"It belongs to a *what?*"

"Oh, there are other names," Durante said: "kuntilanak, matianak, langsuir, lamia, lagaroa, asanbosam, for starters. Also stirge, manananggal and penanggalang, chupacabra, strigoi, brahmaparusha, kali, mullo. I could go on because nearly every culture ever to exist speaks of them, but let me put this in terms you'll understand: that book belongs to a vampire."

"You've got to be—" Dex started to say, thinking this man was a total wacko. But before the last word left his lips, he swallowed it. Those teeth. The bite. "The garlic," he said, paling.

"Protection," Durante said. "One of the few legends that have merit. The silk scarves do the same."

"Why the seeds?"

"Precaution. It is believed that vampires cannot resist counting them. You do not want to be bitten by a vampire, my friend. And not because of the ridiculous stories about becoming one yourself."

*"Disease,"* Dexter whispered

Durante nodded. "Is that what—?"

"There's no garlic outside," Dex said, his pulse surging. "Those guns, and that man downstairs, with the bottle. You—you want her to come here!"

"You've seen it!" Durante cried, suddenly animated. It was like he'd finally been plugged in and could use the muscles in his face. "Tell me what you know!"

Dex hesitated, so Durante rushed at him. He grabbed Dexter's bandaged hand and began to squeeze it.

Dexter, in instant agony, screamed out, "I killed it!"

Now Durante's face froze. He dropped Dexter's hand. "Imposs—" he said, but was just then interrupted by a man bursting into the room. It was Conrad, the guy from the van who'd dragged Daphna away. He was wearing a flight suit.

"Sir!" he panted. "The girl! She's gone!"

"What?"

"Broke the window when I stepped out. I saw her running toward the woods."

Dex could hardly believe it. He was delighted, but also scared and confused. That didn't sound like his sister at all. Maybe they'd tried to hurt her. He'd kill whoever it was.

"Let's go," Durante said. He turned to the goon who'd just been standing there the whole time. "Stay here," he said. Then he was gone.

"Guess she's the tough guy," the goon sneered, dropping lazily onto a couch.

Dexter didn't reply. He couldn't speak anyway with his heart burning in his throat. He moved to the window. Men were sprinting out across the field.

"Guess you two aren't that close, eh?"

Dexter knew it wasn't like that. Daphna was up to something. She'd gotten her courage up and found a way to distract everyone. He had to be ready for whatever she had in mind. She wouldn't just leave him there—not if they lived a billion lives.

Dex watched the men now dashing through the trees. But then he saw something else, directly below. Daphna! She wasn't in the woods at all. She was there, running away! Instinctively, Dex stepped close to the window. She was being chased by Conrad! She must have fooled him somehow. Dexter barely restrained the urge to call out to his sister. She was running toward the helicopter! *What was she doing?*

Conrad was gaining as they neared the aircraft. He had something in his hand. His gun!

He shot her.

An image, worse than his worst nightmare, took shape: Daphna flying—her body suspended in the air over the parched field for an impossibly long time—then falling face first into the ground. She lay motionless, lifeless. Now the guy was hauling her body up and shoving it into the copter.

"Noooo!" Dexter screamed.

The goon leapt off the couch. Dexter whirled around and made a break for the door. He knew it was locked, but he was going to rip it off its hinges with his bare hands.

No, he was going to run right through it. Dex hurled himself into it, taking the brunt of the impact on his chin.

"Not the clever one, either," said the goon, but Dexter didn't hear it.

# CHAPTER TWELVE
*Airborne*

Somebody was shouting.

Daphna opened her eyes and, for just a moment, thought she was in Heaven. Everything was bright, blaring white. But the scene quickly resolved itself. She was in an ambulance, white walled and fitted with all white equipment. Computer screens, I.V. bags, and medical contraptions of various shapes and sizes were attached to the walls. The only color she saw came from lights blinking at her in pale reds and blues. She'd been lying halfway under another collapsible stretcher, next to a puddle of vomit.

It was so loud.

Yes, it was an ambulance, but an ambulance in a helicopter.

Daphna realized she'd been lying with her face mashed into the metal floor for some time. Woozy and aching, she sat up, wiping her mouth with her sleeve.

Conrad, now wearing his helmet, was shouting into a microphone stalk. "All of them?" he cried. "Are you absolutely sure?" Then, "It wasn't there either? Is he still alive? What about the boy?" He turned as he was speaking and saw Daphna blinking at him. "I'm out!" he said, then waved her forward.

Carefully, barely able to keep her balance, Daphna climbed into the co-pilot's seat. Her head, once again, was absolutely killing her. Once settled, she immediately fastened the safety harness over her chest. Then she noticed the view and momentarily forgot everything. They were soaring over Oregon, and it took her breath away. The sheer volume of green, a vast terrain of trees blanketing hillsides in every direction. It was an awesome sight. But then she came back to her senses.

Conrad was waving at her, pointing to the floor between the seats. Another helmet was lying there, so she picked it up and put it on. It was way too large and wobbled overtop of her skull. He also handed her a bottle of water and a protein bar.

"I know you heard you aren't sick," Conrad said after she'd chugged half the water and ripped into the bar. His voice filled Daphna's ears under the helmet. "But I can't confirm that yet. Durante's tests may not be reliable."

"What do you mean 'not reliable'?" Daphna asked.

"I don't work for Durante."

"What?"

"I'm a federal agent. About a year ago, I infiltrated his operation. I'm Agent Conrad."

"Federal agent?" Daphna repeated dumbly, frozen mid-chew.

"Virgil Durante is a dangerous man."

"Wait—you're rescuing me? What about my brother!"

"I'm only rescuing you out of necessity," Conrad said. "Durante has zero tolerance for incompetence in his employees. With the knife and the phone, I was worried you were going to blow my cover. I had to get you out of there."

"Why didn't you just tell me you were a federal agent? Why did I have to think you were going to kill me!"

"I'm sorry, Daphna. But in my experience, kids are unpredictable and fear is the best motivator. I thought you might insist that we bring your brother out if I told you who I was."

"But—!" Daphna was furious and full of anguish about leaving her brother behind, but she didn't really have an objection to this. It was true. Instead she asked, "What—what are you investigating Durante for?"

"Virgil Durante is an eccentric with unlimited resources to indulge his little hobby," Conrad explained. "We're watching him for any number of violations. For one thing, he has no regard for international health regulations. If he thinks there's fairy dust in the remotest part of the Amazon rainforest, he'll raze the whole thing to get it and then ship it here, heedless of possible diseases he might spread."

"Is he crazy?"

"Possibly. He's certainly monomaniacal in his pursuit of occult objects."

Daphna looked out the window at the green of Oregon flying by beneath them for a moment, then turned back to Conrad. "I've learned that people who seem evil or crazy usually have a reason," she said. "You just have to know a lot about them to understand why they do what they do."

"Well, that's rather wise for your age," Conrad replied. "Durante has certainly had a tumultuous life. Quite the mix of good and bad luck."

"What do you mean?"

"He was born rich—never had to work a day in his life. Was an only child and highly introverted. Seems to have spent most of his childhood studying with world-class tutors. He got interested in philosophy in high school, then went on to study it in college. After graduating, he launched the largest atheist organization in the world."

"*Atheist?* But if he doesn't believe in God, he surely doesn't believe in all this"—Daphna wasn't sure what to call his interests—"evil supernatural stuff."

Conrad nodded. "He shut down the organization after his wife and son died."

"Oh, my gosh," Daphna said. She suddenly felt awful for the man. "What happened?"

"They died in childbirth."

"Oh, my gosh," Daphna said again. "Were there really bad complications or something?"

"Just bad luck. There's a shot women get, to ease the pain—"

"An epidural."

"You sure know a lot for a kid. Anyway, in a very small percentage of cases, the woman can develop an acute condition of fluid in her lungs. She couldn't be resuscitated, and they couldn't save the baby, either. It's extremely rare for both to die, but it does happen."

Daphna didn't reply to this at all. It was too awful to contemplate.

"It was front page news at the time," Conrad continued. "Durante sued the nurse who administered the shot. He sued every doctor in the room and on the case. He sued the doctors' supervisors. He sued the hospital administrators. He sued everyone remotely connected to the procedure. Word was he spent over ten million dollars on legal fees."

"What happened?"

"Nothing. It was nobody's fault. One of those bad things in life that happen for no reason. When it was over, Durante closed his organization and, for whatever reason, started his fanatical collecting. He wouldn't hesitate to turn the whole world upside down and shake it until everything he's after falls out. We think this book he took from that abbey—the book we now know originally belonged to your adoptive mother and was brought back to her just before you called 911—may contain microscopic bacteria, virulent bacteria, powerful enough to start a pandemic."

"If you knew what was happening at the abbey, why didn't you stop it!" Daphna demanded, thinking the world was already upside down, like Brother Joe's cross. "Why didn't you call for help? You could've gotten the book, and Dex and I would both be safe!"

"We didn't know," Conrad explained. "What I just told you we pieced together afterward. I'm just one of Durante's lackeys at this point, and obviously not a very good one. All I knew at the time was that an artifact he greatly desired was within his reach after he intercepted some secret electronic communication.

"It's my job to watch all of his procurements because most of them are illegal in one way or another. We don't act on them because we're building a case. Anyway, by the time I alerted my team to what was happening at the abbey, it was too late. When they got there, the place was empty, save for a slew of discarded robes and one fatality."

"Brother Joe?"

"What's that?"

"The fatality! Was it a monk? In an office! Brother Joe is dead?"

"I don't know. But Daphna—"

"So go in now!" Daphna was outraged and disproportionately upset to hear Brother Joe might have been killed. Was he dead when she'd collapsed on him? He seemed like a nice man—a librarian! "Go into the lodge!" Daphna shouted. "Get the book and get my brother!"

Conrad didn't reply at first. He seemed to consider his response. Finally, he said, "We can't yet. We need to know for sure what we're dealing with. It's been hard to find out anything useful about the book from Durante. Like I said, he's eccentric. He thinks it belongs to a vampire."

"What?" Daphna cried, yet again. She wanted to laugh, but then it hit her. Those teeth. The bite. But there was no such thing as vampires! But there was no such thing as almost everything in her life. Was Dex going to be trapped there now? She felt like throwing up again.

"Are you okay?" Conrad asked. "You took a nasty spill and more than likely have a concussion."

"*Bats,*" Daphna whispered, ignoring this. *All that garlic,* she thought.

"What's that?"

"Nothing," she said. "The book is not contaminated. Dex and I both touched it. A lot. Just go in and rescue him!"

"The fact that you are not ill doesn't prove the book is clean."

This gave Daphna pause. She hadn't thought of that.

Were they just lucky? But no, she knew where the disease came from. She wracked her brains for what she knew about vampires. Nothing really, but words were just words—one person's vampire was another one's demon. "Look," Daphna insisted. "I can tell you one hundred percent for sure that the book isn't infested, or infected or whatever. You can go in and get my brother."

"How's that?"

"Something bit my—Evelyn. I saw it. Dex and I both saw it."

Conrad turned to look at her, brows raised.

"Ah—it was—a bat," Daphna said. "In the basement."

"A bat," Conrad said. "Are you absolutely certain?"

"Yes."

"And it escaped?"

"No. You don't have to worry about the disease spreading. Dexter killed it. He stabbed it with a broken piece of metal while it was biting her."

"Then where was the bat? No animals were found at the scene."

"I don't know!" Daphna snapped. Why was he making this so difficult? "I'm telling you," she insisted, "it's dead. The disease isn't going to spre—"

Daphna's voice died in her throat. They'd been flying over Portland for a while now, which she'd observed only semi-consciously. But now she recognized her southwest neighborhood. Multnomah Village was small enough to see in its entirety. Consequently, so were the emergency, police, and military vehicles that had it completely surrounded. Orange sawhorses barricaded every street leading out of the area, and every one of them was guarded by green-clad soldiers with guns. There were other people there too, who seemed to be carrying signs. Everyone's face was covered one way or another.

Unable to speak, Daphna could only turn to look at Agent Conrad.

"Bat or no bat," he said, "your mother has all three forms of the Plague. It's in her lymph nodes, it's in her blood, and it's in her lungs. The infection is airborne—and it's already spreading."

# CHAPTER THIRTEEN
### Code Six

An earsplitting signal suddenly blared from inside the lodge, shocking Dexter out of semiconsciousness. The goon jumped over him to yank open the door, then ran out of the room.

Dex didn't move. His ears were ringing, and his entire face felt caved in from crashing into the door. Why had he done something so stupid? He just lay there and listened to the rushing about, thinking that something significant must have happened, but he couldn't quite remember what it was.

"Code Four! Code Four!" someone was hollering.

With the help of the closet door, Dex got to his feet. People were running back and forth in the hall. He turned and walked to the window, thinking there was something outside he needed to check on.

Dex stood there, rubbing his chin the way he'd seen that zillionaire freak rub his huge neck. But there was nothing going on there. No—something was happening in the woods. There were men among the trees, all standing rigid, all touching their ears. Dex knew what this meant now. Then, at once, they started sprinting back toward the lodge. When they neared it, some of them fanned out around the building, taking up defensive positions with guns drawn, both regular and weird types. The rest rushed inside.

Guns. Did Dex already know they had guns?

Nothing happened then, except lots more shouting and running around downstairs. Dexter's presence had apparently been forgotten.

Some of Durante's men outside tucked themselves behind the pillars that supported the lodge's tiled awning. Others crouched behind the decorative trees just in front of it. Was he being rescued?

A dust storm was rising in the distance. Vehicles approaching. Moments later, they were there, a convoy of luxury cars, skidding and sliding as brakes were slammed. No sooner had they stopped, the passengers were out and running toward the lodge wielding wrenches, tire irons and, from the looks of it, anything else they had in their cars. Someone had an umbrella. Dex knew who they were well before he saw the masks.

*Those are some angry animals,* Dex thought.

The hierarch in his silver cassock and white sneakers was in the herd, moving somewhat slowly toward the lodge's front doors, but the whole mob stopped and fell back when the guards stepped forward with guns leveled at their hearts.

Shouts were exchanged, but Dex couldn't hear them. He still couldn't remember whatever important thing it was that he needed to remember. He wanted answers, and he wanted them now, so he headed out of the room to figure out a plan, and when he saw the two large vases holding some kind of cacti on tables near the elevator, he knew what to do. Dex grabbed one, rushed back into his room, and threw it through the window.

The dispute outside ceased at the sound of breaking glass. The cactus fell to the ground, and its vase exploded in the midst of Durante's men, who wheeled around and aimed their guns up at Dexter. *Was there already broken glass down there?*

"Where's my sister!" Dex shouted. But everyone immediately turned their attention away from him.

"Give us the Book!" the hierarch demanded of Durante's men, whose guns were pointed back at him again. "You fools have no idea what you are dealing with!"

Just then the door below opened, and Dex saw Durante walk out. He stepped calmly around the debris and approached the hierarch, who, though tall, he dwarfed. But before Durante spoke, the alarm sounded once again.

Durante spun around.

A man in rectangular glasses came running out of the lodge. "Code Five!" he shouted, "Code Five!"

Durante spun around again, this time scanning the scene beyond the invaders. All the guards were doing the same. And now the Cartographer's Guild followed suit. Dex as well. No dust was rising from the road.

"There!" someone yelled, one of the guards, pointing at the forest.

Out of it emerged a squadron of police in shiny yellow suits. There were dozens of them, some with riot shields, others with what looked like high-powered rifles, all with large tanks on their backs and full-hooded masks over their heads.

Dex knew he should be ecstatic, but something told him things were about to go from bad to worse, and that there was something extremely important he was still failing to re-member. At least the ringing in his ears was starting to fade.

"Drop your weapons!" one of the cops boomed through a megaphone. "Drop your weapons and lay face down on the ground! Do it NOW!"

The hippos and crocodiles obeyed.

Durante's men hesitated, but when the order was re-peated as the officers fell upon them, they put down their guns and cooperated too.

Durante, himself, did not. He remained where he was, standing among the prone bodies, masked and unmasked, surrounded by highly armed police. But he was visibly unim-pressed. Dex could see the lack of concern in every bit of the man's bulky body.

"Get down!" an officer in charge shouted at Durante. "Now!"

Just then the alarm sounded for a third time.

Half a dozen of Durante's men burst out of the lodge this time, all crying, "Code *Six*! Code *Six*!" They were immediately grabbed and thrown to the ground.

Dex could tell from the desperation in their voices that there was no Code Seven.

Durante stiffened and turned toward the satellite dishes still rotating on their trucks. Then he looked up at the sky, which was darkening in an unnatural and terrifyingly rapid way. The cops looked up as well. Bodies on the ground rolled on their sides to see.

But now there was nothing to see because the darkness was already nearly total. It was as if a shovelful of dirt had just been dumped on the sky.

And it was freezing cold.

"We're too late!" someone screamed. One of the Guild. "The creature is upon us! Run for your—!"

The last word was swallowed by the sound of flapping wings, a storm of flapping wings that seemed to choke the air itself. Bats were suddenly everywhere.

But no sooner had they appeared, they were gone.

And then the winds came.

A massive gust of brutal, hot, sick-smelling wind slammed the grounds. The entire lodge seemed to shudder from the blow.

Dex leaned through the window frame, straining to see. Everyone had been toppled but Durante, whose silhouette was fighting its way through the black wind back into the lodge. Dexter thought he heard the sound of tires squealing as cars sped away.

When the screaming started—soul wrenching screaming—Dex turned and walked out of the room. The moment
he stepped into the hall, the power went off. For an instant,
it was pitch black in the lodge, but then it lit back up. There
were emergency lights mounted on the walls. Dex hadn't noticed them before. He was standing two feet away from the
guards posted along the balcony railing. They were aiming
their bizarre nail guns below, directly at the glass cubical in
which the endless pages of the Book of Maps were still being
scanned.

*Is this really happening?* Dex wondered, looking down
over the rail at a half dozen men on the floor surrounding the
cubicle, all with guns poised.

Durante was standing on the hearth once again, arms
crossed, his face in a line, rubbing his neck while the screaming continued outside.

He swept some seeds onto the floor with his foot, then
went still again.

No one moved.

Then, like a plug had been yanked from a wall, the fren-
zied screaming outside stopped.

There was silence.

The men with guns tensed.

Durante waited.

And then there was music. Flute music. The man who Dex
had first seen standing next to Durante was playing his flute,
walking in slow circles around the glass cubicle. The bottle
hanging from his neck no longer had its cork in it.

And then the mist swept in.

And then something was there.

A figure in a white hooded cloak stood in the center of
the room, directly next to the book. It seemed to be consider-
ing the nature of the cubicle that contained it.

Dex couldn't move. He knew he should run, but he also
knew he wouldn't until whatever was going to happen, happened.

The man with the flute kept playing, a plaintive tune, cir-
cling the monster now, drawing closer with each cycle round.
The thing seemed to take no notice of him, though, even
when he got within arm's length of it.

But then, suddenly, two hands shot out from the cloak.

They disappeared an instant later.

The music was gone. The bottle shattered. The flute play-
er was on the floor, his head turned nearly all the way around

his broken neck.

Dexter saw Durante nod.

Nails ripped through the air from every angle around the room. Silver blurs streaking toward the monster, striking it over and over again with a dozen, a hundred, a *thousand* fleshy smacks. The creature fell into a crouch, shielding itself from the onslaught.

"The neck!" Durante roared as the nails continued to fly. "The back of the neck!"

Dex's heart pounded hopefully, but only until it dawned on him that the thing wasn't screaming this time. The nails weren't working. It had to be a talisman. Durante didn't know about the talismans.

"Now!" Durante cried, and a clear box of some sort, the size of a phone booth, fell from the rafters directly over both the thing and the book in its cubicle. The booth began to fill with smoke, smoke rife with the powerful odor of garlic. The smell was so strong that everyone began to cough. But everyone was also cheering.

For sixty seconds, the smoke pumped into the booth, but then it was turned off and the lodge went silent. Nothing inside the box was visible but white, plumy fumes.

"Lift it," Durante ordered. "Lift it!"

The booth rose slowly, raised by thin cables that Dex, of course, hadn't noticed.

Durante looked up and saw Dexter standing like a stone at the banister. He smiled—a giddy predator's grin—then turned back to his prey. Dex wondered when and if the man had ever smiled before.

The smoke was clearing quickly now.

When it dissipated completely, Dexter was the only one not surprised to see the thing was no longer crouched on the floor. She was standing, fully at ease. Nails lay in heaps at her feet among the seeds. Her hood was still on, but she turned her face toward him, and now Dexter was perhaps the most surprised person there.

It wasn't her.

It was a man, a tall, pale man with the same blood-red lips. He was just as beautiful as she, in a masculine way, but also just as ugly and appalling.

He was simply standing there, as if alone in his own private library, flipping through the Book of Maps. The box it had been in was in pieces.

Durante gaped at the vampire he'd lured into his trap. He clearly did not know what to do now that it had failed. He was simply staring at it with a mix of horror and fascination. "I knew it!" he suddenly shouted as his men began backing slowly toward the exits. "I knew it! I knew it!" he cried, grinning now like a father who always knew his child could succeed.

Apparently oblivious of Durante, the vampire continued flipping through the pages, his hands moving at blinding speed. Dex had followed the men to the lower level and waited for his turn as they began slipping outside. And now the men just in front of him were at the door. Seconds later, the last of them was gone.

But Dexter didn't follow. He was captivated by the blur of pages still whipping through the thing's hands. *He's looking for something,* Dex realized.

"Whatever you're looking for, I can help you get it," Durante said. He was still on the hearth. "I have unlimited power among men."

The vampire stopped flipping pages and looked up. He seemed surprised anyone was there. It smiled jagged yellow teeth. "Now let's not exaggerate," he said in a voice that was deep, melodious, and veined with untold centuries of life. Then he looked down at the page he'd stopped on. "Ah," he said, and in a simple, casual motion, tore it out. The bookmark Daphna had discovered fluttered out of the book. The vampire folded the page in half, then slipped it into his cloak and looked back at Durante.

"Look down," Durante said. From his angle, Dex could see he had something behind his back. A wooden stake.

The thing looked down. Dex did too. *The seeds.*

But the thing looked back up, laughing a deeper version of that demonic laugh. "Stories," it said. And then, in an instant, it was on Durante, having traversed the distance between them too quickly to see. The stake went flying and the towering man was in the air, held up by the neck.

Dex simply watched this horror, waiting to see the thing's teeth sink into the billionaire's flesh, or to hear the bones in his neck snap when his head was wrenched off. But suddenly, blood spurted from Durante's throat like water from a ruptured pipe. Evidently disgusted, the vampire tossed him away like a dirty rag. Durante's body hit the floor heavily. It quivered a bit as blood pooled around his head.

Dex didn't move. He didn't remember how. The thing turned and regarded him again, but just then someone stumbled into the lodge.

The little hippo in the oversized suit.

"I beseech thee!" he cried, throwing himself upon his

knees. He raised a cross in self- defense, but his hands were shaking so badly that he dropped it, chain and all, to the floor.

"What is this?" the vampire asked. He was standing in front of the quivering hippo, holding the cross. His voice showed no hint that he'd been involved in any sort of physical struggle seconds before.

Durante's body was still.

The creature pulled the cross off its chain and looked closely at the hole in its base.

"Don't hurt him!" Dexter cried.

The next thing he knew, it had him by the throat. He'd been lifted half a foot off the ground and was literally flying backwards as the creature charged forward with him in his grasp. Dex's skull and spine crashed into the wall. He was hanging there, like a doll in a child's grasp. But he wasn't afraid. He wasn't even there. He was being choked by some-one else, somewhere else. Who was that? He was up against a tree somewhere. In the park?

The monster opened its mouth and Dex knew that he would die. And he knew why he hadn't fled when he'd had the chance. He had neither fight nor flight left in him.

Daphna was dead.

Dex wanted to be too. They could be perfected togeth-er. He closed his eyes and waited to be released.

But the thing did not bite him. It dropped him. Then it moved swiftly back to the center of the room, grabbed the little hippo, and dragged him out the front door like he was no more substantial than an empty robe.

Dex ran to the door. There was nothing there but a foul mist departing on the breeze.

He sat down and cried.

# CHAPTER FOURTEEN
## Neck and Neck

In a heap, half in and half out of the lodge, Dexter wept. No thoughts were registering. His entire self was dissolving, pouring out of his eyes.

"Is it gone?"

Dexter stopped crying and looked up, shocked to hear Durante's perfectly calm voice. The man's blockish head had popped up from the heap he was in and was looking Dex's way. Then he sat up.

"What—how?" Dex asked.

Now Durante sprang to his feet like a fallen athlete miraculously ready to return to the game. The display of agility was at complete odds with the lugubrious way he'd moved until then. Durante's neck was a gruesome mess. He put his hands on it, feeling it side to side. Then he reached around behind his head. There was a tearing sound that made Dexter's cringe. He watched in horror as Durante seemed to peel the flesh right off his throat.

But then Dex understood. It was fake, some kind of false skin that bled.

Rubbing his real neck, the man surveyed the shambles that had been his headquarters. He looked anything but displeased. In fact, he was beaming. Eventually, he noticed Dexter staring at him. "Always anticipate the worst possible outcome," the billionaire said, his voice alive again, as it had been when he'd nearly crushed Dex's bad hand. "That's Rule Number One," he added, stepping lightly into the litter of workstations and computers to pick up the Book of Maps.

"You lost," Dexter said, confused by Durante's bizarrely victorious mood. "No Count Dracula for the old museum." Not that it meant anything to him anymore. It felt good to say, though.

"Lost?" Durante asked, amazed, or amused. *"Lost?* On the contrary!" he cried. "The veil has been lifted at last! I've seen the other side, and soon the rest of the world will too!" His previous face seemed to have been paralyzed. This new one flashed what looked like every possible permutation of pleasure. Durante tossed the Book into the debris.

"You don't want it anymore?" Dex asked. Something stirred in him, a possibility.

"Small potatoes, it seems," Durante said, setting one of the desks back on its legs.

"What do you mean?" That book, whatever it actually was, had to be the most incredible object in the world. "He came for—Oh." Dexter remembered now. It had torn something out. The page with writing on it.

Durante had set up an overturned chair and was now putting a laptop on the desk. "He wants something else," Durante said. "But I'm going to find it first, and that's how I'll get him."

Dex got up and walked over to see what he was doing. "Why?" he asked.

Durante looked surprised at the question and stopped what he was doing. Then he said, "There are more things in heaven and earth, Horatio, than are dreamt of in your philosophy."

"What?"

"Shakespeare," Durante explained. "The fountain of truth." Then he turned back to the computer and started clicking. Maps began flashing on screen at a dizzying pace. The scans of the Book. He was looking for that page.

A second later, it was there. Durante clicked a few more times, then looked up. "Right," he said. He found a printer on the floor and restarted it. A page came out a few moments later, which he looked over, then folded in half much the same way the visitor from beyond the veil had only minutes before.

"What is it?" Dexter asked.

"Coded no doubt," Durante said. "But I'll crack it." He tucked the printout into his jacket pocket, then headed for the steps leading upstairs.

Seeing him walk away snapped Dexter out of the nowhere state he'd slipped into again. "You killed my sister," he said before Durante had gone two steps up. Locking eyes with the man, Dex added, "One day, I'm going to kill *you*." As soon as the words left his lips, he knew he still had a reason to live.

"What's that?" Durante asked. He looked genuinely shocked.

"Your man," Dex explained. "Conrad. The pilot. He shot my sister. She didn't run into the woods. She was running away after your men went looking for her. He shot her in front of the helicopter, then shoved her inside."

Durante's brow lifted itself on his blockish forehead. "If this is true," he said, "he shot her despite my explicit instructions not to harm her. He was going to the university hospital in Portland, OHSU. If he shot her unintentionally, he may have taken her with him to save her to avoid my wrath." His voice was not without sympathy. "He better have," Durante added.

Dex didn't reply. The blood that had dried up in his veins was suddenly flowing again.

"I have no use for either of you now," Durante added. "But I'm heading to Portland and will take you there if you like. I'll need to clean up and get my things first. Would you like a lift?"

Dex nodded. He was ready to run to Portland on his own two feet, but this obviously made more sense. "There are two of them," he said, feeling like he ought to give something back.

"Two of what?"

"There's a female," Dex explained. "I injured it. Maybe really bad—I don't know."

"How did you manage that?" Durante's keen brown eyes zeroed in on Dexter's reply.

"I stabbed it with something. Something that monk had. The really fat one. It was a piece of metal with some kind of writing on it, I think."

"Where is it now?" Durante asked, leaning into the banister as if to get hold of the answer quicker.

"It melted after I stabbed her," Dex said.

Durante's face sank, but he nodded, a quick gesture of gratitude, then walked up the stairs. He stopped again, though, and said, "I'll need to be off the radar for while. I'm going to leave my clothes in a pile on the floor up here and change. You might want to leave yours as well. Grab any backpack under the tables in the back. It's bound to have a fresh set of clothes."

Dex nodded now. Off the radar sounded like an excellent idea. A question came to mind, so he asked before Durante disappeared onto the upper floor. "Why are you interested in vampires, anyway?"

Durante smiled. "I'm not," he said. And then he was gone.

*"Me neither,"* Dex whispered. He spotted a bag, but did not approach it. It could wait a few moments. First, he got the Book. Then he hurried over to the laptop still displaying that page of text.

He found the print command in one try. Not even his eyes would dare mess with him right now.

# CHAPTER FIFTEEN
### The Greatest Gift of All

"In cases like this," Conrad explained, "we seal off the infection zone and start immunizing everyone in and around it. The circle widens if it spreads, until we contain it. Unfortunately, no one's ever seen a strain of Plague quite like this, so we're not sure the vaccine will have any effect at all."

Daphna hadn't asked a question. She'd been rendered mute by the sight of her neighborhood looking like it had been taken over by an invading army. She saw her own house cordoned off completely by yellow tape, like it had been the scene of some ghastly crime.

They were above the southwest hills now. Daphna could see the complex of university hospital buildings they were aiming for. Conrad honed in on one, and slowly brought the helicopter down toward its roof. As they got close, Daphna saw a fairly large crowd of people there, apparently waiting for them.

A number of them were cops. And every one of them was holding handcuffs at the ready.

"You lied!" Daphna screamed. "You're not going to let me go!"

"Calm down," Conrad said, concentrating on the landing.

"I didn't scare you into rescuing me!" Daphna cried, suddenly seeing what happened at the lodge more clearly. "You wanted to get me out of there the whole time! The lamp was the only thing not bolted down! You had set it up before I ever threatened you!" They were on the roof now.

"We had to get you out of there without tipping Durante off," the double-crossing secret agent calmly explained. "The real truth is that we need to talk with you both, to go over every detail and analyze every possibility. You have no idea how bad this might become. And like I said, until we test you ourselves, we can't rule out the possibility that you and your brother are infected. So we *will* need to get Dex out and test him too—but later. I'm sorry, but taking you both out was just too complicated and risky. We figured Durante would be satisfied with Dexter while we dealt with you."

"I'm not going into that hospital!"

"You'll be in good hands," Conrad promised. "Dr. Fludd will stop at nothing to get to the bottom of this. She's probably the most well respected scientist in the world right now, which is why officials at the highest levels of government are working with her. That's how serious this is. She is relentless. In fact, she's famous for working twenty hours a day since she was in college. If you or your brother are infected, she will cure you."

The crowd outside, cops and medical personal, were approaching the helicopter, but Conrad held up a hand to say they should wait.

Daphna was nearly apoplectic. "You lie!" she screamed. "You're a liar! Everyone lies! I refuse to—!"

"Your brother is missing."

"What?"

"After we left, something happened."

"What are you talking about? What happened!"

"The team was forced to move in. A competing faction arrived and initiated direct conflict with Durante's men."

"The Guild?" Daphna cried. "Were they wearing animal masks?"

Conrad nodded. "The team moved in to secure the situation, but—"

"But what?" Daphna demanded. When Conrad failed to answer immediately, she begged, "Please don't say winds."

"Some sort of weather anomaly," Conrad confirmed. "A sudden storm of some sort. It's not entirely clear what—"

"Where's my brother!"

"No one was there."

"Were his clothes there?" Daphna asked. Her voice had gone calm, almost soft. But her insides were shriveling.

Conrad looked at her with an expression that gave away nothing. "There was a T-shirt just like yours," he said.

Daphna's face went slack. She took the helmet off. The propellers had come to a stop. She stared out the windshield with no comprehension whatsoever of anything she saw.

"We need your help, Daphna," Conrad said, his voice calm and encouraging. "You may be the key to preventing a catastrophe."

Daphna did not reply. She did not move. She did not hear.

"I knew I could count on you." Conrad waved to the men and women on the roof. He opened his door and jumped out. Someone opened Daphna's and helped her down. She did not resist.

Daphna was guided across the windswept roof, down a stairwell and through a series of shiny hallways. At some point she was handed off to a woman wearing a disposable cap, mask, gown, and gloves. Her voice was urgent, commanding—though Daphna heard not a word she said. Her legs moved, but on their own. Her brain was not sending any signals she was aware of. It seemed like they were walking forever though hallways, but it didn't matter.

Nothing ever would again.

At some point, Daphna heard a word: "mother."

She stopped. "My mother is dead," she said.

"No," said the woman, pulling her along now by the arm. "Your mother has made an unexpected turn for the better, just today! She may be responding to the experimental treatments I've devised. I've even been able to take her off the ventilator. Only, she won't answer any questions about this book. She's only said that you kids weren't there and don't know anything about it, which is why we didn't come looking for you right away. But we know you were there now. A security camera in a store across the street showed you and your brother out on the sidewalk talking to Abbot Augustine just before that wind burst shorted it out. We know he brought the book to your mother. We'd like you to talk to her. See if she'll tell you what she won't tell us. Do you think you could do that?"

Daphna nodded.

Then there was more walking, more stairwells, more halls. Everyone they passed was wearing the same disposable outfits. Some of them had guns. Someone called the woman "Dr. Fludd," and everyone backed away when she drew near.

They went down a dozen more gleaming white halls and stopped at a door.

"Go on in," said the world-renowned Dr. Fludd. "In the first room, you'll find a set of protective clothing. You'll put them in the disposal box on your way out. Don't be alarmed by the large machine inside. It's cleaning the air."

Daphna pushed open the door and stepped inside the vestibule. The change of clothes was sitting on a padded bench. She ignored them.

Evelyn was on a bed. She was wearing a surgical mask over her nose and mouth, but it didn't hide the fact that her face was now completely covered in awful black splotches. Her neck was impossibly swollen. The rest of her—a skeleton it seemed—was under a blanket. Wires of all sorts seemed to be running under it from a number of large and frightening machines that could have been in a science fiction film. A loud hum was coming from some kind of contraption the size of a refrigerator with blinking lights. The filter, Daphna assumed. At least this place seemed to know what it was doing.

Slowly, Evelyn's head turned toward her visitor. Glassy eyes took Daphna in.

Daphna rushed to the bedside and took her adoptive mother's hand. It was shaking terribly. "Evelyn!"

*"I've so hoped to see you,"* her second mother whispered, her ravaged voice barely audible, *"to say goodbye. I*—I told them you weren't there. I expect you are fighting it. Dexter—is he here?"

"No," Daphna said, whispering back. "But he's—he's okay." There were no tears, and there would be none. Never again.

"Good," Evelyn sighed. "Good."

"That book," Daphna said. "Does it show the ways to Heaven? I need to know. I really need to know."

Evelyn's eyes shone with compassion. "The maps are false," she croaked, her voice like air leaving a balloon. "A diversion."

"A diversion?" This couldn't be true. It was all Daphna had left.

"Did you ever wonder how I never lost track of Adam— your father—for centuries after he sent me from Eden?"

Daphna blinked at the question. She knew that Evelyn had radically changed her looks, even her body shape, to enable herself to keep meeting him anew, but no, Daphna hadn't wondered how she'd never lost him. "How did you do it?" she asked. "With the maps in the book?"

*"No,"* Evelyn whispered. There was an awful rattle in her voice that was painful to hear. "I used a gift given to me by God," she said, "a gift that would let me find him no matter where he went—and to know I was not alone—a gift of the most precious object in the universe." Evelyn paused and struggled for a breath that seemed just beyond her. Then she whispered, *"This gift could never be lost, so he gave me a book that would always take me to it in whatever way I required, a book that anyone would think was the gift itself. I never lost the gift, but for a short while I lost the Book of Maps—a disaster."*

"Babel?" Daphna asked, and Evelyn nodded. "What was the gift?"

But before Evelyn could answer, all the machines in the room began beeping at once. Evelyn seized up off of her bed for a moment, then fell back down, gasping.

The door burst open and suddenly the room was full of medical personnel.

"The gift!" Daphna cried. "What was the gift?" She fell to her knees so her face was near Evelyn's. Someone was trying to pull her away.

Evelyn's eyes opened. Her mouth moved. Only the feeblest noise came out, but it was enough. "*Aleph*," she whispered.

Daphna was dragged away, but she witnessed the moment Evelyn's eyes—the eyes of the first woman ever to behold this world—closed, once and for all.

In the crush and confusion of doctors and nurses tending to Evelyn, Daphna tried to slip away. But she got no more than a few steps down the antiseptic hallway before a guard grabbed her.

Her aversion to violence ended then and there.

She threw kicks and punches. She scratched, aiming for eyes. She bit. She ripped hair. More than one person was on her now, but Daphna struggled for all she was worth. Eventually, of course, she was overwhelmed. Three men had her pinned to the hard floor.

"Daphna!" a woman was shouting, but she was still raging. "We need your help!" It was Dr. Fludd. "We need your help to figure out what killed your mother! We need your help to find your brother!"

"He's dead!" Daphna shrieked. "Everyone I've ever loved is dead! I won't help you! I'd rather die! And the whole world can die too, for all I care!" Daphna had no control over any part of her body but her mouth, so she spit—poisonous venom she hoped. She spewed fire.

Dr. Fludd nodded. Someone squatted down next to Daphna. She felt a pinch in her upper arm.

As everything inside her mind went dark, she prayed it would be forever.

# CHAPTER SIXTEEN
## *Wheelng & Dealing*

Durante drove his own limo, and he let Dexter ride in the back. Upon climbing inside, Dex, for just a moment, reveled in the luxurious interior. He'd never been anywhere near a limousine, let alone inside one. It was all leather and decked out with full entertainment and information centers. After raiding the mini fridge and snack bar and stuffing himself with deli sandwiches and chips and soda, Dexter—despite the alternating highs of optimism and black fits of fear that battered his brain—passed out on one of the long soft seats. He woke up at seven o'clock feeling like a new person. Evening was settling over the sky as they sped along.

Dex thought he made out a Portland sign. He knew he had to make some decisions, and quickly. So he did.

Off the radar was out. He was going to make a deal—if there was something to deal for. If not, well, it wouldn't be his concern anymore. Nothing would.

There was a cell phone plugged into a charger mount, so Dexter picked it up, activated the voice control and asked for Oregon Health Sciences University. Once he was connected, he had only to say his name before he was put through to someone sounding official.

"Dexter," a woman said sternly. "We need to know where you are right now. This is very important. People are sick and we need—"

"Where is my sister?"

After a moment's pause, the voice said, "She's here."

"You saved her!"

"Saved her?"

"Did nothing important get hit?" Dex had heard of people who survived being shot because the bullet passed right through without hitting major organs.

There was another pause, this one longer, after which the voice said, "Dexter, she might not make it. She's been asking to see you. Will you come in?"

This time it was Dexter who paused, his suspicions now

aroused. "Did you get the arrow out?" he asked.

"It was difficult, Dex," the woman replied, this time immediately. "It caused some significant internal damage. I don't mean to scare you, but you really should come see her as soon as possible in case—"

"You're lying," Dexter snapped. "She's not there at all!"

"No! Dexter! Don't hang up. I'm sorry. I—I don't know how to talk to children. I've never—She *is* here. She wasn't shot. She came in on a Life Flight helicopter with a federal agent. She's fine. She has a nasty bruise on her forehead from a fall. We just need to see you. We need to run tests. You and your sister were exposed to a deadly disease. Blood tests and X-rays show Daphna is not infected, but you may very well be. Your mother—I'm sorry, Dexter—she did pass away today. Daphna saw her before she died."

How easily Life and Death toyed with Dexter Wax.

"I have the Book," Dex said, thinking about how he'd said nothing to Evelyn as she lay on the basement floor, struggling to live. *Nothing.* "I'm willing to give it to you if you let my sister go and leave us both alone," he added. "We're not infected—Did you say *federal agent?*"

"Dexter, we need that book. And we need *you* too. You might have critical information that could help me find a cure. This is not a game. I only want to help you. Do you understand that you might be dying?"

"I'm hanging up now."

"No! Please don't. I'll release her. This is a big mistake, but I'll do it. How can we get the book?"

"When I see my sister, and we know she wasn't followed, I'll call you and tell you where it is. If we see anyone, I'll let it rot until it infects the whole universe."

"What has happened to you kids?"

"What?"

"You don't mean what you just said."

"Let her go or you'll find out how much I did."

"What should we tell her?"

"Just tell her I'm skipping school." Dex hung up without waiting for further response.

"Outstanding work," Durante said, his voice startling Dex from hidden speakers. "Really, I'm very impressed. Professionally done. If you want to work for me someday, a job is yours."

"You—you were listening?"

"Of course," Durante said. "I was hoping you'd take the Book and make that call."

Dex shook his head. "That's why you told me where they

went." Was he always going to be so easy to manipulate?

"I wasn't sure that imbecile was a mole," Durante said, "but now I understand a few things. You've done me another favor, so I thank you. But I'll be keeping that Book. It will come in quite handy."

"Can I ask you something?" Dex asked. Durante could have the stupid book. What did he care?

"Shoot."

"If you believe in vampires and all that stuff, why not Heaven too?"

Durante laughed at this, a good hearty laugh. "You're young," he said, "but I suspect you've seen a few things. Tell me, which is more likely, vampires and all that stuff, or Heaven?"

Dex didn't answer. "All those things you collect," he said, "for your museums—are any of them real? I mean—"

"Every one."

"Oh."

"Or are you asking me if I've ever actually seen a magical object in action, or witnessed a supernatural event, or encountered an otherworldly being before today?"

"Well, yeah."

"No," Durante said. "I haven't."

There was something in Durante's voice—a tortured strain—and it forestalled any further questions. Dex didn't really know what made him bring that up anyway. "Can you give me a ride to Gabriel Park?" he asked.

"Ah, scene of your previous crimes, eh?" Durante chuckled. "Very good, sir. I'll have you there straight away."

# CHAPTER SEVENTEEN
*Very Much So*

"Mom?"

Someone was gently shaking Daphna, drawing her out of a deep and satisfying sleep. A voice was beckoning. Was she late for school?

But the fog was clearing quickly in her head, and the darkness poured back in. She opened her eyes.

It was Dr. Fludd, whose face Daphna could now see for the first time. She was middle aged, with fierce, penetrating eyes and shining black hair. She looked tired, very tired. "Daphna," the doctor said, "you can go."

"What? What time is it?"

"It's eight o'clock. Daphna, you can go. Your brother called us. He has the book and offered it to us if we let you go. So—despite how foolish this is—I've decided to take the deal."

Daphna shot upright. "Dexter's alive?"

"Apparently very much so."

"What—where is he?"

"He told us to tell you he was skipping school. Don't worry, we're not going to follow you. A cab is waiting. We drew some blood and took some X-rays. You are not infected, but we don't know about your brother, who could be out there spreading the disease. And we must have that book. I've worked too long and too hard to get where I am. There is no way I will allow religious fanatics, bored billionaires, or two foolish kids to get in the way of me preventing this pandemic."

Daphna wasn't listening. Despite the heaviness in her limbs, despite yet another anchor on her brain, she was already off the bed and scrambling to get out of the hospital gown she found herself in. Her clothes had been set on a chair.

When she was dressed, Dr. Fludd walked her back through the gauntlet of security guards, through the maze of halls, and to an elevator. Even though she felt like the walking dead, Daphna had to force herself not to run.

"You two may eventually face charges," Dr. Fludd said as they rode the elevator down.

"We've faced worse," was Daphna's cheerful reply.

# CHAPTER EIGHTEEN
### *A Hand with Hebrew*

Dex was lying in the leaves, staring up at the only star visible through the leafy ring of treetops overhead. He hadn't been in the Clearing since last year, since the day seven brave people were murdered here over another impossible book. He'd thought about them once in a while, but they'd long since blurred even in his excellent memory into one ancient person, one wise old person he'd never become. Dex thought about Emmett and Asterius Rash and his parents. And now Evelyn, kind, sweet Evelyn, the woman who'd given them their lives back. So many people gone—simply *gone*—from the world. Where were they? Was there such a thing as Heaven? Did their souls exist somewhere?

When that monster finally killed him, Dex wondered, where would he go?

Dexter watched as a few more stars came out, seeing them as ancient people must have, as portals to places beyond. Were the dead up there somewhere? It was stupid to think they were running around on clouds, but there was something about the sky.

After an hour—Dex watched the night cover the park like a hood—he became certain he'd been tricked once again, that his sister was as dead as everyone else in his life. He contemplated digging a hole right there and just jumping into it.

Then he heard a tentative snap in the woods.

"Daphna!" he cried, scrambling to his feet.

If it was a trap, it was a trap.

"Dexter!" her voice cried back.

She materialized among the trees, spotted him, then ran right at him. Brother and sister embraced in the center of the Clearing, laughing and hugging in an explosion of tears.

"I'm so sorry!" Daphna sobbed. "I never should have left you! I broke my own promise! I'm sorry. I'm so sorry. I'll never, never, never do it again! They lied to me! They said they found your—where's your shirt?"

"I wanted them to think it got me," Dex explained, looking down at the olive green T-shirt he'd taken from someone's bag, but then he said, "I thought he shot you! Running toward the helicopter!"

Daphna had to think a second. "No," she said, putting two fingers to the lump on her forehead. "No! I fell! I tripped and hit my head! I threatened to tell Durante that he let me use my phone. He smashed it. I thought I scared him into saving me so I could get help, but he's a government agent! They have no idea what's really going on, Dex. The whole Village is blockaded because of Evelyn's infection. It's spreading. They think it's all from the book. I didn't tell them anything. She wouldn't have believed it anyway."

Dex shook his head at these developments. He'd seen all kinds of flashing lights from the limo. Durante avoided them, but still managed to get near the park on Vermont Street. Dex filled his sister in on the events that took place at the lodge.

"There are two of them!" Daphna gasped. "A *male?*"

"It grabbed me by the neck," Dex said. "It was going to kill me. But, it didn't. I don't know why. The Guild was there. Maybe they got away. I don't know. No one was outside when we left, no clothes or anything. The thing took one of them away with it—that short one who found the book under the desk, I think."

"Took him away?" Daphna asked, shuddering. Then she remembered more of her own awful news. "Brother Joe!" she cried. "Conrad—the agent—he said someone was dead at the abbey, but he didn't know who it was. It had to be Brother Joe!" Daphna sank to the ground, overwhelmed by so much death. Dex joined her, and they sat in silence for a few minutes, listening to the night sounds among the trees.

"I haven't been here since—" Daphna croaked.

"Me neither."

"Evelyn is dead," Daphna reported, flatly. "I saw her die."

Dex did not reply. He lay back on the leaves and looked up at the sky again, into the darkness that stretched into infinity. His sister lay back next to him. After a minute, he told her about his conversations with Durante on the ride to Portland.

"So, let me get this straight," she said when he'd finished. "Almost being killed by a vampire made him *happy*. It, like, cured his depression."

"Pretty much. I think he might not have actually believed in any of the stuff he collects until now. He definitely doesn't believe in Heaven."

"Well," Daphna said, "the Book of Maps is fake."

"How—how do you know?"

"It's a decoy, I guess—all this Heaven stuff. The maps—or

that page maybe—it shows the way to something Evelyn has, in case she lost it, something that helped her keep track of Dad all those centuries. She called it an aleph."

"The Hebrew letter on the cover of the Book of Maps!"

"Right!"

"Oh, my gosh," Dex said, sitting up. "I totally forgot." He took the scanned page out of his pocket, even though it was far too dark to read. "This is it," he said. "The page it tore out. Durante found it on his computer, from all those scans. I got a copy. He thinks it's in code."

"We need some light," Daphna said, sitting up as well. Energy was suddenly starting to flow again. "If that's the key part," she added eagerly, "it has what we need to know in a way we can understand. Well, in a way Evelyn could understand, but maybe it'll work for us too. Great job! We should have read it when we had the chance!"

"Where can we go?"

"The Village is like a ghost town," Daphna said. "The only lights I saw were street lights, but the cops are out patrolling everywhere."

"When Durante drove me in," Dex said, "we saw a bunch of people. They looked like they were protesting at the border of the Village—down there on the other side of the post office parking lot, right out on the street. Maybe we can slip into the group and use the light there."

"Let's try," Daphna said, getting up. "Worst comes to worst, we run for it and meet back here. Then we'll make a new plan."

"Deal."

So the twins headed back through the woods and, once out, found the path they needed out of the park. Dex didn't even look at the tree where this all began for him. They walked without talking, without thinking. Once they reached the bordering street, they considered the houses lining the opposite curb. Excepting the last, none had a single light on. No cars were in driveways. The area looked pretty much deserted.

"*Come on,*" Dex whispered. The houses all backed up to the post office's parking lot, so the twins crossed the street and slipped between two of them. Each had a fenced back yard, but the one on the left's was rotting and cracked—there were plenty of gaps to see through.

Crouched in front of the largest hole, Dex and Daphna saw that the lot was filled with police and medical vehicles. There was even a military truck, the kind with a large green tarp tented over the back. Beyond that, they could just see through to the street, where sawhorses blocked the way into Multnomah Village. Voices were audible from the barricade, shouting voices.

"This doesn't seem like such a good idea any more," Daphna said. "It looks like they're using this as some kind of operations center. Lights are on inside."

"But no one's in the lot," Dex pointed out. He pulled at the rotten board they were peeking through with his good hand, and the board started to come free. Daphna helped him pull it all the way off. The space wasn't big enough to fit through, so they worked a second board loose and peeked through. It was true, the lot was quiet.

*"They're all out patrolling the streets—like you said,"* Dex whispered. "The lot looks empty. Let's duck down and cut through."

Daphna reluctantly agreed, so the twins slipped through the fence, crossed a grassy divider, and snuck into the lot. They scuttled between cars, getting as close to the protesters on the street as they dared. The vehicle nearest the scene was the army truck, so they hid behind one of its huge back wheels and peered over.

There were men in army fatigues out there, but the people shouting were civilians, maybe two dozen, holding signs. Everyone had medical masks strapped over their noses and mouths. The streetlights were bright over the scene.

"No Occupation!" they were shouting. "No Marshall Law!"

*"Daphna,"* Dex whispered.

"Government Lies Make Us Sick!" someone chanted. There were other cries in the hubbub:

"Mercy for the Dying!"

"Prepare for the End of the World!"

"Daphna!"

"Justice is at Hand!"

"What?" Daphna turned, annoyed that Dex wasn't letting her figure out how they were going to slip unnoticed into the protest. But then she saw how white her brother's face was. He'd pulled back one of the canvass flaps that covered the back of the truck and was pointing inside. Daphna looked.

Coffins. Plain wooden coffins. Dozens of them.

Before Daphna could react, an altercation started on the street. Dex let go of the flap and he and Daphna looked up. A group of men among the protesters, all dressed in dark suits—jackets and ties—were trying to force their way past the barricade. The soldiers pounced on them at once, but the twins saw, the moment the melee commenced, another figure in black, this one bearded and elderly, emerge from behind a small apartment building across the street, inside the Village. He walked calmly, but swiftly toward the fracas. No one saw him. Once he reached the intersection, he walked around the sawhorses, took off his medical mask, then began to call for calm.

The men stopped struggling at once. The guards began to cuff them.

"Please!" the old man cried. "I am a rabbi! These men are my students. We apologize. We will leave at once."

The guards looked at one another and apparently agreed it wasn't worth dealing with some kind of religious incident.

"Get going. Now," one of them ordered. The group immediately fell in behind their rabbi and began following him down the street. They passed directly in front of the twins.

"Dex," Daphna whispered as they moved past. "Rabbis speak Hebrew. Maybe he can tell us what the aleph on the cover of the book means. Maybe he can help us with the page!"

"Let's go."

With heads down, the twins hurried back through the lot as the men walked parallel to them on the street. They re-entered the backyard they'd spied from and slid up along the side of a house until they could see the street again. The group had turned the corner and was walking their way. The twins were safe in the dark, though. Even if the group entered that exact house, they wouldn't be seen.

Virtually right in front of them, the men stopped. Handshakes were exchanged, and then everyone headed off into the park. Everyone but one. The rabbi remained on the street, watching his students depart. When they were gone, he headed down the sidewalk. The twins stepped out into the front yard, just far enough to see him enter the last house, the one with lights on. They waited until he'd gone inside, then hurried to his door. Dex pressed the buzzer.

It opened almost immediately. The rabbi was apparently expecting one of his students, because he said, "Nu? What now?" before he saw who it was. Then he looked surprised and confused. His beard was flecked with gray, and he had a pleasant, chubby face. A black skullcap sat atop his head. His eyes were droopy and encircled with dark rings. He looked a bit out of breath.

"Mr.—Ah, Rabbi—sir," Dex stuttered, unsure what the proper greeting was. "We're sorry to surprise you like this. At night. We were hiding, and we saw you coming out of the

Village. We have friends who live in the area—"

"And you are afraid for them. Please," the rabbi said, "come in. Come in. Let me get you something to eat."

"Oh, you don't have—" Dex started to say, but Daphna cut him off.

"Actually, that'd be great," she said. "I'm kinda starving."

"Please, this is no problem," the rabbi assured her. "You are my guests." He bade the twins to follow him inside. The entry hall was lined with books on plain pine shelves. Oriental carpets covered the hardwood floor. Oddly, on the wall between two shelves was something large in a frame that was draped with a black sheet. As the rabbi led the way through the long hall, the twins both stared at it. He showed them into a room, a warm, wood-paneled study. Another frame hung on the wall inside, also draped in black.

"Please, make yourselves comfortable," the rabbi said, pointing to two chairs covered with tattered maroon upholstery. When the twins obliged, he hurried out.

"*What's with the sheets?*" Daphna whispered, tipping her head at the draped frame. The rest of the room brimmed with books.

"*I don't know,*" Dex whispered back. "But I'm dying to know. It's like that missing painting in the museum you told me about, the empty spot people stared at for so long."

"Yeah, exactly. Anyway, Dex, how exactly are we going to ask for his help without sounding like a couple of lunatics?"

Just then, the rabbi reappeared bearing a plate with a cut apple and a fanned out stack of crackers. Daphna took it gratefully and started to munch. Dexter passed.

"My name is Rabbi Tanin," their host said, taking a seat behind his desk. Neat piles of papers and books sat atop it here and there, along with a computer and a small printer. A tall lamp with multi-colored glass sat next to the chair. "I've been trying to find out the truth behind this quarantine, myself," he continued, "and to see what help is needed. Many members of my congregation live inside the zone, and it's unacceptable not to know how they are. This supposed 'precautionary measure' is a lie."

"What did you find out?" Dexter asked.

"All lines of communication to and from the area are down. Land lines, but cell towers are dark too. Satellite service for computers as well. That's why we know they're lying. They don't want the truth of whatever's going on here to be known."

"What *is* the truth?" Daphna asked.

"People are sick. Of this, there is no doubt. There are signs on some doors, big Xs. Everyone is afraid to come outside. It is positively medieval! And I have learned they are planning to sneak coffins inside!"

Dex and Daphna exchanged a glance.

"Something awful is going on," Rabbi Tanin said. "I won't lie to you."

"Thank you," Daphna said, swallowing her third apple slice. "We really appreciate you telling us this. It's hard to find the truth anywhere these days."

"It's hard to find anyone who seeks it," the rabbi replied. But then he added, "It's really not safe, even here for you. I am an old man—"

"We heard you were a rabbi—outside," Dex said, trying to delay their dismissal and come up with a plausible story at the same time. "We've also been trying to find something out that you might be able to help us with. For school—a project about World Religion."

Daphna nodded enthusiastically. The good old Project Excuse. "Yeah, a summer project," she added.

"I'll do my best," Rabbi Tanin promised. He looked pleased, perhaps to leave the worries of the real world behind for a bit.

"An aleph is the first letter of the Hebrew alphabet, right?" Dexter asked.

"Indeed it is."

"Does it mean anything else?"

"Of course!" the rabbi replied. "What doesn't? In Hebrew, each letter is assigned a numerical value. There is a longstanding tradition of trying to find meaning in the mathematical relationships revealed when words are converted to numbers. Aleph represents the number one, or one thousand when used at the beginning of years. It also often stands for all the letters at once."

Dex and Daphna looked at each other to consider this jointly. It seemed like something, though they didn't know what.

"Have you ever seen a symbol," Daphna tried, "with an aleph in the middle of a really fancy compass rose, with arrows pointing out in almost every possible direction?"

Rabbi Tanin looked thoughtful. He ran his hand through his beard and leaned back into his chair, which creaked rather noisily in protest. "No," he finally said, "I don't believe so. But it puts me in mind of the 'aleph numbers.' They are used in a branch of mathematics called set theory. I'm not very familiar with it, but I think they are used to represent the size of infinite sets."

*Infinite.*

This was *definitely* something, but neither Dex nor Daphna knew whether they should keep asking questions or risk showing the rabbi their page.

"In mystical Judaism," Rabbi Tanin continued, evidently just warming up, "the letter stands for the *Ayn Soph*, which means, literally, 'without end,' representing both the singularity and boundlessness of God. Let's see," he went on, stroking his beard again, "the shape of the letter itself is said to represent a man pointing between Heaven and Earth to show that the lower world is the map and mirror of the higher. Does any of this help?"

"Yes!" the twins assured him. They silently urged each other to ask the next, crucial question, but neither could come up with it.

"Is there something else you'd like to know?"

"Ah," Daphna said, "this might sound like a dumb question."

"Ask! My students should be so dumb!"

"In Judaism," Daphna ventured "is there anything like, say, a crystal ball, something to help you see things maybe far away?"

"Alas, no," the rabbi replied.

It seemed like the twins had learned all they could without simply handing over their precious page, but neither of them had the nerve to risk that, so they just sat there in an uncomfortable silence, willing each other to salvage the situation.

Daphna noticed her brother worrying the now tattered strands of his gauze wrap and came up with a plan to both stall and strategize a bit more. "I don't mean to impose, Rabbi Tanin," she said. "I mean any more than we already have. But by any chance do you have gauze and some Vaseline?"

"Daphna," Dexter moaned.

"That thing is a disaster," she replied. "We haven't been able to take care of it."

"That bandage is a fright," the rabbi agreed, leaning forward to see the pathetic thing. "How did you hurt your hand?"

"I burned it," Dex replied. He hadn't thought about his hand in a while, which had been a good thing.

"Please, absolutely," the rabbi said. "One moment." He got up and headed into the hall.

As soon as he'd gone, Dexter scowled at his sister.

*"Dex,"* Daphna whispered, ignoring the look. "I only want-ed to get us some time to talk for a second. We've just spent the last fifteen minutes lying through our teeth to a rabbi. First a monk, and now a *rabbi!* But I'm afraid to give him that page. He might think we're crazy and tear it up or something."

"We've got to keep asking questions," Dex insisted. "He has to know more that could help us."

"I don't know what to ask!" Daphna cried.

"I want to ask what's under those sheets."

Rabbi Tanin came back in with a roll of gauze. "I apolo-gize that I have no ointments," he said, waving Dexter over to his desk. "My household is not in the best order lately."

Dex decided he had no choice, so he walked over, giv-ing Daphna his nastiest glare along the way, even if it had been a good way to buy them time. But she was staring at the black sheet now. Reluctantly, he gave the rabbi his hand.

Rabbi Tanin noticed Daphna's blatant staring as he un-wound Dexter's wrap. "My wife recently passed on," he ex-plained. "It is traditional to cover the mirrors in the house for the duration of the mourning period. It's long past time to re-move the covers, but the truth is, God forgive me, I sometimes imagine I can see her face in the depths of the—" The rabbi stopped mid-sentence. He lifted Dexter's now fully exposed hand, and peered down at it with a curious eye.

"What is it?" Dex asked, worried. "An infection?"

Daphna hurried over to look too.

"Please, one moment," the rabbi said, reaching with his free hand into a desk drawer. He drew out three tangled pairs of glasses, which he dropped on the desk. He shook one pair loose, slipped them on, then leaned over the hand again.

Dex stared down at his palm. There were welts raised on the skin. They looked random at first, but then actually maybe more like—"

"My God!" Rabbi Tanin exclaimed. "That's Hebrew!"

# CHAPTER NINETEEN
### Between the Lines

*"Hebrew?"* Dex asked. "What do you mean?"

"A burn, you say? This is a burn?"

"Yeah. It was on a piece of metal. It got really hot—What does it say?"

"Where was this piece of metal?"

"Ah—ah," Dex stuttered.

"It was in a museum," Daphna said. "Do you know who Virgil Duran is? The mega rich guy with all those weird museums?"

*"Durante,"* Dex corrected.

"I know of him, yes," the rabbi said, "from the news. I am not surprised that he would have such a thing. How did you come to be burned by it?"

"We were up there, in Seattle," Dex said, pleased with Daphna's quick thinking. "With our parents," he added.

"And there was this kid there, playing jokes on people," Daphna put in. "He thought it would be really funny to move the piece—it was like a shard or something—onto a stove they had to keep something boiling."

"Witch's blood."

"Yeah, witch's blood. It was really corny. Then he knocked it on the floor and got Dex to pick it up."

"Despicable," the rabbi said. "Both this boy and this museum."

"What does it say, anyway?" Daphna asked.

"Let us finish, and I will explain." Rabbi Tanin gave Dexter a new wrap, then sat back down at his desk. The twins sat down again as well. This new development was totally unexpected, but extremely welcome. "The word on your hand," he said, "is *Senoy.*"

"What does that mean?" Dex asked.

"Of course, a long story," the rabbi replied. "Do you know anything about the Garden of Eden?"

"Yes!" the twins blurted together, nearly leaping out of their seats.

"I mean, we do—quite a bit—I mean, we know some—"

Daphna fumbled, eyeing her brother, scarcely able to control the sudden surge of excitement these words caused. "From our class," she hastened to add.

"I'm so glad to hear it," the rabbi replied, smiling again. "Have you ever actually read the story," he asked, "as it is set down in Genesis?"

Daphna nodded. She'd read it dozens of times.

"Perhaps you noticed then, something strange about the account of the creation of the first people."

Dex hadn't read it, of course, but he remembered spying on Daphna's class last year. "There are two different versions," he said. "One says Adam and Eve were created together, and the other says Eve came after Adam, from his rib."

"Wonderful!" Rabbi Tanin cried, evidently delighted to see religious learning in young people.

"Which is proof that everything the Bible says can't be literally true," Daphna added. "That's what Mr. Guillermo said last year."

"Ah, but it proves no such thing," the rabbi said, smiling. He looked delighted to have a debate shaping up.

"What do you mean?" Daphna asked. "Both can't be true. It's impossible."

"Allow me," the rabbi said, reaching to a shelf behind him for, the twins assumed, a Bible. "Sometimes we must read between the lines to find the truth," he said, flipping to one of the first few pages. "The first account takes place on the sixth day and is as follows:

"'And God said, 'Let us make man in our image, after our likeness. They shall rule the fish of the sea, the birds of the sky, the cattle, the whole earth, and all the creeping things that creep on the earth. And God created man in His image, in the image of God He created him; male and female He created them."

"Right. That's the passage people interpret to mean they were created together," Daphna said.

The rabbi turned his attention to the facing page. "The second account," he continued, "is as follows: 'Lord God formed man from the dust of the earth. He blew into his nostrils the breath of life, and man became a living being.' It goes on to explain how God made the Garden of Eden and brought all the animals and birds for Adam to name. Then it states:

"'For Adam no fitting helper was found. So the Lord God cast a deep sleep upon the man; and, while he slept, He took one of his ribs and closed up the flesh at that spot. And the Lord God fashioned the rib that He had taken from the man into a woman; and He brought her to the man.'"

"I don't get it," Dex said. "Unless they don't mean what they sound like they mean, Daphna's right: they can't both be true."

"Why not?"

"Because Adam and Eve can't have been created together *and* separately."

"Dex," Daphna said, the wheels turning in her brain, "what if it's not talking about Adam and Eve both times?"

"Are you saying there were two separate creations?"

Rabbi Tanin beamed. "Many scholars believe there were two creations," he confirmed. "They believe that Adam had a wife before Eve."

"What?" Daphna asked. She'd not come across anything like this. She hadn't read enough!

"She is called *Lilit,* in Hebrew. There is no direct evidence of her in sacred Jewish texts, yet she does appear in the tradition, and has played a significant role in Jewish fears over the centuries."

"Who—what is she?" Daphna asked.

"The myth originates in Sumer," the rabbi explained. "She was a type of wind or storm spirit, called *Lilitu,* thought to be the bearer of death and disease. How appropriate to be talking of her now, given the situation outside."

The twins locked fearful, certain eyes for a moment, then turned back to Rabbi Tanin.

"It is generally, but by no means universally believed," he continued, "that Lilit refused to serve Adam, and was subsequently banished from Eden, after which she became a demon that prayed on babies and men, like a type of vampire who craved human blood. In fact, there is little doubt that she is the source of all vampire myths. Today, the feminists hold her up as a model of female independence." He chuckled at the thought. "But there are other theories entirely," he added.

"What are they?" Dex asked, trying not to shout.

Rabbi Tanin got up from his seat and approached a neatly arranged bookshelf packed with old tomes. He ran his finger along the bottom shelf until he found what he was looking for. "As you may know," he said, "there is ample evidence that God was willing to start over when things in his world went wrong."

"The Flood you mean?" Daphna asked.

"Precisely. And let me tell you another brief tale from the tradition." The rabbi was flipping pages, but spoke while he searched for whatever he was looking for. "When the universe was first created," he said, "the sun and moon were of equal size and brilliance. But the moon demanded that God diminish the sun so it could rule the sky. Instead, God punished the moon for its greed. He stripped layers of crust away until it was small and dim, then banished it to the night—Ah!"

The rabbi stopped and scanned a page he'd found, then looked up. "Yes," he said, "I thought it was here. There are some who believe the first account of creation, in which man and woman are created together, is quite literal."

"What do you mean?" Daphna asked.

"That God's first Creation was a creature both male *and* female. I believe there are some who propose that this first creature was also part animal, and could take the shape of natural elements as well—which provides us with a nice connection to the wind spirit myths."

"So, could it be female at one time and male at another?" Dex asked.

"Why not?" Rabbi Tanin said. "An interesting idea."

"And," Dex added, a thought leaping out from the tangle in his mind, "the animal part. What if it was a—"

"Snake," Daphna said, right there with him.

Rabbi Tanin looked positively enchanted. "That is wonderful!" he said, clapping hands. "There is a long-honored Jewish tradition of proposing stories to fill in the gaps of sacred tales. You two show much promise!"

"So—so," Daphna said, her mind racing alongside her brother's, "Lilit could have known Eve, but Eve might not have known Lilit, if she was a snake, I mean. In the Garden."

"Wonderful!"

"So God got rid of her—or it," Dex asked, "and started over with Adam and Eve?"

"So some believe," the rabbi confirmed. "God is said to have felt his creature was far too powerful, that Lilit challenged *Him*, not Adam, and that is when God decided to separate these powers: male, female, animal, and element." Rabbi Tanin scanned some more of the book he held, then added, "Lilit was banished from Eden and warned never to interfere with humans. She had a chance for a separate, if diminished existence, like the moon, perhaps."

"But she did—interfere—with Eve, right?" Daphna asked.

Rabbi Tanin read a bit more. "Perhaps so," he said, "because she was later condemned to dwell underground, in the caves outside of Eden, and told if she continued to violate God's wishes, she would be sealed there forever, or until the day the Word of God set her free."

"*The Word of God,*" Daphna whispered. She looked at Dex, who nodded sadly. God was long gone before Babel, let alone the time of the Aztecs and Incas, but his rules evidently still held sway, which was somewhat comforting. Lilit had indeed interfered with humans—who knew how many times, enough to become a legend all around the world—and she, or he—or it—had finally been sealed underground. But the Word of God did set it free—a single word of Power from their own lips, spoken to save themselves from falling into her prison.

"This word on my hand," Dex said, trying to focus on the present. "What does it have to do with all this?"

"In ancient times," Rabbi Tanin explained, putting the book away, "it was traditional for Jewish parents to hang an amulet around the neck of male infants. These were inscribed with the names of three angels: Senoy, Sansenoy, and Semangelof. If I recall correctly," he added, "the original amulet, forged by the High Priests, was broken and lost. It is believed that they have the power, not just to ward Lilit off, but to kill her completely. No doubt your Mr. Durante claims to have found one of the original pieces."

"Thank you," Daphna said. So now, at last, they knew what they were dealing with.

"*Oy,*" said the rabbi, looking at a clock on one of the shelves, "it is nearly ten o'clock! Your parents must be worried! Is there anything else I can help you with?"

"One more question," Daphna said. "We really appreciate your time. Would Lilit want anything? I mean besides human blood? Would she be looking for anything?"

"I know nothing of this," the rabbi replied. "I'm sorry."

"That's okay," Daphna said. She turned to her brother and nodded.

"I have one more question too," he said. He stood up and took the scan out of his pocket. "You were talking about reading between the lines and how words can be worth numbers and all that. I was wondering—are there ways to decode entire stories?"

This brought one more smile to the rabbi's face. "We look for meaning many ways," he said, "because the mysteries of the Torah are inestimable. Its deepest mysteries are secret, revealed only to those who learn to see them, to those ready to receive them, and to those for whom they are intended."

The twins were jolted by this last comment.

"We're wondering if there's a secret message in this," Dex said. He handed the paper to the rabbi, who took it with interest. He laid it out on his desk, then leaned over it. The twins pulled their chairs up close.

"There was once a poor man who climbed down to his cellar to retrieve coal for the fire he needed to keep warm. Finding he had none, he lay down in despair and fell asleep. In his dream, a voice instructed him to journey to a kingdom far away, for there, buried in a cave on the grounds of the King's palace, he would find a great treasure. The dream returned every night until, finally, the dreamer could ignore it no more. The poor man spent his very last coins on a map and set out to find his fortune.

"For many months, the man traveled, enduring every manner of hardship along the way, but at last he reached the kingdom he sought, and soon after he found the caves on the palace grounds. The area, however, was guarded day and night. Every day the poor man lingered near the caves, hoping for an opportunity. Eventually, he grew so hungry and weak that in desperation, he began to eat his map. Seeing this, one of the guards grabbed him and demanded to know his business, thinking him insane. The poor man, nearly delirious, blurted out the story of his dream and the journey it inspired. When he finished, the guard burst into laughter.

"'What a fool you are to believe in dreams!' he roared. 'Why, if I gave credence to such nonsense, I would be well on my way to the city you've come from. For just last night I dreamt that a poor man there has a treasure buried in his cellar under an empty coal bin. Now get out of my sight.' The poor man bowed and immediately began the long trek home, guided by the scraps that remained of his map.

"When at last he reached his humble home, he dug in his cellar, under the coal bin, where he found the treasure he'd been searching for."

Dexter, who'd been staring at the page with wonky eyes, said, "I've heard something like that before. It was a picture book some teacher read one time. The lesson was, you have everything you need already and don't need to go looking for it."

"I remember that," Daphna said. "I also think there's something like this in *A Thousand and One Nights*."

The rabbi, nodded, pleased again. "There are versions of this tale in evidence from cultures all over the world," he told the twins.

"What do you think, Rabbi Tanin?" Daphna asked. "Is it in code?"

The rabbi looked the page over again, then said, "I see

no obvious enciphering, but there could be a thousand and one ways to hide a message here. In a good cipher, often the words themselves have no meaning, and the message lies beyond them, between the lines as I said. Scholars spend lifetimes studying the sacred words of the Torah, often finding nothing."

"Lifetimes?" Daphna said, impressed but also disturbed. "Why do they keep it up?"

"The promise," Dex answered, staring again at the blur of ink on the scan. "You said it yourself," he added. "People are more interested in what they can't see than what they can—like that painting again—and the mirrors. We couldn't stop wondering what they were."

"Dex, you're totally right."

"You are remarkable children," the rabbi observed. "Truly re—"

"Can I borrow those glasses?" Dex interrupted, his face suddenly aflame.

Rabbi Tanin was taken aback by the question and didn't respond at first. Without waiting for permission, Dex picked up one of the two pairs remaining on the desk, a pair of sunglasses with yellow lenses.

"Dexter!" Daphna scolded.

"Do you have a pencil?" Dex asked, ignoring her.

"What are you doing, Dexter!" Daphna demanded. But then she caught on. "Wait," she said, "the tinted lenses! What do you see?"

"Hold on," Dex said. He held a hand out, but did not take his eyes off the paper. The rabbi put a pencil in his hand.

Dexter began writing on the page. Daphna leaned in close to see what he was doing. He wasn't writing. He was shading the space between two letters. Then he did the same between two others.

"Between the lines," Daphna said softly. "The string—the crazy string you see."

Without looking up, Dexter said, "Some of the letters and words are spaced farther apart than others." He was shading furiously now, before he lost what he could see.

Fascination spread across the rabbi's bearded face as he watched.

When Dex had all the spaces filled in, he turned to his sister. Even with the glasses, it didn't look like anything much to him.

But it did to her. She took the pencil and connected the spaces by drawing right through words when necessary.

When she was done, the three of them beheld the result.

"Wonderful!" the rabbi cried, clapping his hands. "You are angels sent to divert me in this difficult time!"

"What is it?" Dexter asked, squinting at the page.

"Numbers!" Daphna cried. "Dex, you are a genius!"

"But what do they mean?"

The twins turned to their host, who shrugged. "Who knows?" he said. "Decimal numbers, it seems."

"Actually," Daphna said, "they look like the numbers I was watching on the GPS."

"We need a map!" Dex nearly screamed. He looked immediately at the computer sitting atop the rabbi's desk.

"By all means," Rabbi Tanin said. "I love to look at the satellite pages myself!" He turned and moved the mouse, which lit the screen. He clicked on something that opened a webpage, then chose a bookmark, which immediately began calling up a satellite imaging service. Daphna was already on her feet standing behind him. Dex got up to join her.

"Read me the numbers," the rabbi said, so Daphna did. When they were entered, he hit "Return" and sat back.

An image of the Earth came onscreen, and it immediately spun to the Western Hemisphere. It paused a moment, then centered on North America.

Dexter and Daphna were barely breathing.

North America enlarged until the United States was featured, which turned toward the West Coast.

The West Coast enlarged until the Pacific Northwest was center screen. Then Oregon.

"How about this?" the rabbi said. "It's coming our way."

The website stalled a bit, delaying the search, but then the map focused on the northwest corner of the state.

Portland.

Suddenly streets were visible, a city view. Highways. Bridges. Rivers.

Now the focus speed was increasing. Streets got larger. Rows of houses appeared.

A single street.

A single house.

"Oh, ho!" the rabbi said.

Daphna was leaning into the screen. Her face was practically on it.

Then she jerked upright.

*"Dexter,"* she gasped. "That's our house!"

"This is your house?" the rabbi asked. "How wonderful! What a puzzle!"

"We have to get home," Daphna said. She and Dex were on their feet. "We have to get home right now. Thank you so much for all your help!"

The rabbi stood up. "This address is in the Village," he said, but the twins were already bolting the room. Daphna reached the hallway first, but halfway down it, Dex tried to overtake her. The result was that they jammed each other into the shelving units on both sides. Books and objects that had been lying across their tops were swept to the floor as they fell.

On their knees, the twins began to scoop things up.

"Please," Rabbi Tanin said, coming out of the office, "don't worry about it."

But he sounded strange, and when the twins looked over the mess one more time, they understood why.

There, half crushed by a heavy book, was a piece of familiar green plastic. Daphna reached over and pulled it free.

A crocodile mask.

# CHAPTER TWENTY
*Benjamin Franklin Saves the Day*

By the time the stunned twins looked back at the rabbi, his face had transformed entirely. With quivering lips and cutting eyes, he hissed, *"The Book will lead us to a better world! I would give my life for it!"*

Dex and Daphna didn't reply. They ran.

By the time the twins reached the end of the street, they realized the rabbi wasn't chasing them, but a police car was coming up the road, so they raced back to the rotting fence.

"How are we going to get into the Village?" Daphna panted when they got there. "I'm sure we can run right in, but all the way to our house? I doubt we'd make it."

Just then, voices.

"How'd we get stuck with this gig," someone complained. A man. There were two men, just to the left of the twins in the lot. They were smoking cigarettes.

"No doubt," the other man said.

"I ain't touchin' no dead bodies, that's for sure. Specially dead by disease dead bodies."

"No doubt."

"We get over to the Art Center. We dump the coffins. We get out. You feel me? Some other chumps can come back and get 'em when they're full."

"I feel you."

"Alright. Let's get suited up."

The moment the men walked away, the twins turned to each other and nodded. Neither had to say that the Arts Center was just blocks from their house—or that they'd found their way home.

Dex slipped through the fence first. Daphna followed him into the lot. This time, they got on hands and knees and crawled between the parked vehicles until they reached the truck.

The twins waited until the moment the men climbed in to stand up and jam themselves through the gap in the canvass door flaps at the back. They'd been in there for no more than ten seconds before the truck lurched backward out of its spot.

It was dark, but the twins scrambled to their feet. *"Here!"* Dex whispered, holding on to two awkward stacks of coffins. He opened one. It looked like there were dozens filling the long cargo space, and they seemed somehow threatening in their silent indifference. Daphna looked at her brother, but did not speak. "Get in," he said. "Just in case. We'll be there in two minutes." Daphna nodded, then climbed in. Dex closed the lid on her coffin, then climbed inside one of his own.

Daphna closed her eyes as the truck bounced over the ramp out of the lot and onto the street. She was strangely calm. She'd always feared she'd somehow be aware, conscious in some awful way, when she was buried. But it was worse to think of the alternative, of not being conscious in any way. When Dex told her to get in, she'd had the instant thought, *No way.* But something whisked the thought away. A coffin, she realized, is the ultimate empty space—or it contained the ultimate empty space: death. Somehow, after everything, she was able to contemplate that space without panic.

But once inside she thought of Evelyn, who'd soon be in a box just like this, if she wasn't already. Her poor mother didn't even get the privilege. The rabbi's last words surfaced in her mind. He said he'd die for the Book of Maps. And she understood the feeling. If she could die to save her mothers—if it was possible somehow to *see* them again—she'd die for the chance. *Hasn't it been two minutes, yet?* Daphna wondered, taking in a long, deep breath. She slowly let it out. Then she took another.

When Dex closed the lid over himself, his mind closed with it. He managed to relax. He'd come so close to dying so many times now that it was almost comforting to imagine the deed was done once and for all. It was tranquil in the box, except for the hum of the motor and the bouncing of the truck, but the combination was almost soothing. Maybe it was better not to fight on and on if what came next was peace…

The truck stopped. Doors opened and closed. The twins began to lift their lids, but there were voices there already.

"Let's do this quick," the more talkative man said, climbing into the truck. "I don't trust these masks. They ain't payin' me enough to catch some Superbug."

The lids went carefully down.

"No argument here," the other man replied.

The twins heard the men heaving out a coffin. Would they notice two were excessively heavy? Of course they would!

They should've jumped out as soon as the truck stopped! Dexter and Daphna realized this at the same time. But there was nothing to be done about it. They'd fight and run. They'd go for the masks.

"This is going to take all night," the talker groused, hauling out the second coffin. His voice sounded as if it had come from right over Dexter's head. And sure enough, a second later, he felt hands on the lid. Dex's every muscle tensed.

"This is really freakin' me out," the talker said.

"Me too."

"What say we speed the plow a bit?"

"How do you mean?"

With that, Dexter's coffin was shoved off its stack. He cried out when his back hit the floor of the truck, but the sound was lost in the noise of the slam. Now he was sliding, and before he could figure out exactly what was happening, his coffin fell out of the truck and onto the ground. It flipped, so Dex's face hit the ground, igniting his jaw again with blinding pain. He could tell his nose was bleeding. And he was trapped.

Now more coffins were being shoved off the truck. Some of them hit Dexter's as they fell off. One of them was Daphna's, he could tell, because he heard her grunt.

"What was that?" the talker yelped.

"What?"

"Thought I heard something."

"Now *you're* freakin' me out."

"Hold on. You move the rest up from the back. I'll check it out."

Dexter pushed on his lid, but it was a waste of time. Should he call out? Maybe spook the men into hightailing it out of there?

Daphna knew what was happening. She tried to brace herself when her coffin started sliding, but when it hit the ground, her head snapped up and then slammed down. She heard a man hop off the truck. He was walking around the pile of coffins now. If he found her, what could she do? Though she'd never use it, Daphna wished she had Dexter's switchblade tucked into her—

Hands were on the lid. Daphna thought she could hear breathing. He must be laying his ear on top, listening. Surely he could hear her heart threatening to explode as she wrenched her hand into her pocket.

The lid opened. Two shocked eyes peered into hers from under a mask. Then they shifted to her hand, which was holding out a trembling one hundred dollar bill.

The eyes looked back at hers, then at the bill, then back again. Suddenly, it was ripped from her hand and the lid slammed shut again.

Daphna could scarcely hear over her own breathing, but during the next fifteen minutes, coffins hit the ground, one after another.

Finally, she heard the truck's doors slam.

A few seconds later, it sped away.

"Dexter!" Daphna yelled, bursting out of her box like a drowning victim from the sea. She was standing in the front lot of the Multnomah Arts Center. It was dark, but a few lights were on inside. Someone was being carried past a window on a stretcher. The building seemed to be serving as some kind of infirmary. *Was that—?* She could swear it looked like her ex-friend, her never real-friend, Teal Taylor's older brother. It had to have been because he looked like a bigger version of Dex. Daphna was suddenly lost in the past, in her old longings. *Was Teal infected too?* But there was no time to wonder. "Dex! Dex!" she screamed.

"Here!" Dex called, kicking at his coffin. "I'm in here!"

He was under the pile! The coffins were unwieldy, but fortunately leaning on each other at precarious angles. Daphna managed to tip enough off to find her brother's.

It nearly broke her back, but she got it turned over. The lid fell open, and Dex rolled out onto the asphalt, sucking in the fresh air.

But it wasn't fresh air. It was diseased.

Daphna put out a hand and helped her brother to his feet. Their eyes met. They didn't bother to congratulate each other.

Instead, and of course, they ran.

# CHAPTER TWENTY-ONE
## Sides

The moment the twins hit the sidewalk, they stopped. There was some kind of ruckus happening down the street. A group of people—a small mob, really, was yelling and banging on the glass of a storefront. The crowd was all kids, neighborhood kids the twins recognized, both hoodlums and Pops.

"Are they near our store?" Daphna asked, hesitantly leaning off the sidewalk to get a better look.

"No," Dex said. "They're *at* our store. They know this all started there."

"Is that Wren?" It was odd to see anyone she knew—it was like real people had simply ceased to exist in the last twenty-four hours. Or perhaps the last year. She was sure that was Wren, but she didn't see Teal.

Before Dex said anything more, one of the kids threw a brick through their window. It was all the twins could do not to cry out.

Someone else started spray-painting on the front door while the others took to breaking out the window entirely. Then everyone stormed inside.

"*Let's go,*" Dexter whispered when he and Daphna were alone again on the street.

Furious, the twins sprinted straight past the store. As they flew by, both got a glimpse of the graffiti just painted on the door. It was a blur to Dex, but Daphna saw it clearly: an upside-down star inside of a circle.

It was only a few blocks to their house.

As they ran, the twins saw doors marked with Xs, apparently with fluorescent tape. Houses were dark all over the neighborhood, and not a soul was out anywhere else. Nothing was moving.

Two minutes later, they were at their house, standing at the front door, looking at the same disconcerting symbol just painted on their store.

"I've seen that before," Daphna said, panting, "in one of my books about religion, but I can't remember what it means."

Dex screwed up his eyes, trying to make it out. "I'm think-ing nothing good," he said. "Let's go." He moved to try the door, but someone suddenly opened it.

The twins leapt back.

"Brother Joe!" Daphna cried. She threw her arms around the surprised and pleased little monk. "What are you doing here?" Thrilled, she and Dex followed him inside. "How did you get past the barricades?" Daphna asked. "How did you survive? I thought you'd been killed at the abbey—in the of-fice—on the floor—you—there was blood—"

"Yes," said Brother Joe, putting his hand to his head. "I must have fallen in the confusion, but it saved my life." He stepped over a broken vase and took a seat on the shredded couch. The living room was still every bit the disaster it had been when the twins last saw it, maybe even worse. "I was the last one left—again," Brother Joe explained. "He—the creature—he believed I had some answers about the Book. Things happened too quickly to comprehend. It swept me up in an icy wind. I couldn't see, but I knew I was moving at incredible speed. When I stopped, I was deep underground. It was so cold."

"It took you to Turkey!" Daphna cried. "To its underground lair!"

"He took someone else too!" Dexter added. "From a lodge we went to."

"The flapping of wings was so loud," Brother Joe said. "There were bats, so many bats—but I did hear another voice."

"Another voice?" the twins asked.

"Yes. A woman, calling for help. I couldn't quite see her. She was there, but not there, like a tormented soul trapped between life and death. Kids," Brother Joe said solemnly, "it was your mother, the one who'd been bitten by the beast. It took her too, from the hospital."

Daphna grabbed her brother's shoulder to avoid collaps-ing. "How—how did you get away?"

"It's ill," Brother Joe said. "Part of it has died. The female part."

"I stabbed her!" Dex cried. "I killed her!"

"It sent me here because it thinks you have the other tal-ismans, and it is afraid. It believes you also have something it wants, something here in the house. I am to offer to trade your mother for it. She can yet live."

"But we don't know where it is!" Daphna wailed, nearly faint with hope. *Evelyn! She could live!* They'd find it and trade it. If the world went up in flames, she'd have her Evelyn back.

"We know it's called an Aleph," Dex said, his heart leaping at the thought of getting another chance to talk to Evelyn. "And it can help you find things somehow," he added, "no matter where they are."

"It's a book," said Brother Joe. "A very small book."

A book. Naturally, a book.

"Hey," Daphna said, suddenly distracted, "there's the book I saw that symbol in!" Despite everything, she was still Daphna, so she had to check it out. She hopped over an overturned drawer, crunching seeds, and picked it up off the floor: *A Beginner's Guide to Religious Thought.* Its pages were mangled, but she flipped through anyway, eager to jog her memory.

"The Aleph," Brother Joe said, turning to Dex, "where could it be?"

"I have no idea," Dex admitted. "The house has been turned upside—"

"Oh, my gosh!" Daphna cried.

"What?" Dex hurried over.

Daphna had found a picture of the very symbol they'd seen both on their store and their house. Under the image of the encircled star was a caption. "Inverted pentagram: common demonic symbol," she read.

*"Demonic?"* Dex sneered. "They think we—?"

"Let me see that!" Brother Joe shrieked, rushing at the twins with his hand outstretched to take the book.

But Daphna dropped it. The page she'd found featured a collection of symbols associated with devil worship, and she'd seen the image next to the pentagram: an upside-down cross.

She looked at Brother Joe, who was blinking at her.

Dex leaned down over at the image, now facing up at him from the floor.

He saw it.

"You were the little hippo," he said, straightening up. "That cross Lilit took—he pulled the chain out of the *bottom*. It hung upside down. You *kept* it upside down."

"You!" Daphna screamed. "It was you!" She backed away from the monk, whose face was twitching. "There was no accident with those moving shelves! *You* killed the old abbot! You killed him so Abbot Augustine would come! You said people thought he was a demon hunter! You thought having him there might lead you to a demon! The door wasn't even locked when we found you!"

"No," Brother Joe swore. He was backing away, stumbling over the litter on the floor. "That's not true. I could never do such a thing."

"You asked for the abbot's phone," Dex said, "but we never told you it was his. You turned on some kind of tracking software, and that's how everyone found the lodge." His voice was calm. Just one more betrayal was all. "You called it when we were under the desk."

"It *is* true!" Daphna raged, her voice like a bludgeon. "That man! In the office at the abbey! He was in the Guild! When he came in to search it, you hit him on the head! You changed clothes with him and that's why the suit was too big! You were that hippo! You lied about hearing a voice in those caves, didn't you! Evelyn is dead! You *wanted* that monster to come! You've always wanted it to come!"

The look of dismay slowly fell away from Brother Joe' face. It was replaced by a cold smile. "And so it has," was all he had to say.

And then the twins noticed the smell.

And then the winds descended.

# CHAPTER TWENTY-TWO
## Gone

"Back door!" Dex shouted.

Daphna looked at him like he was crazy for saying that out loud, but when she saw the smirk on Brother Joe's face, she understood that her brother had a plan.

The twins raced through the living room and into the kitchen. Dex opened but then closed the back door, then tiptoed down the basement steps. Daphna wasn't sure this was a good idea, but she followed him down to his room.

Dex's shaking hand pushed on the hidden door under the steps. It popped open and—

A body fell out.

Rabbi Tanin.

He'd gotten there ahead of them.

Numb now, the twins stepped over the body into the closet and closed the door. There was simply nothing else to do.

The roaring wind had already stopped. Foul, freezing air rushed in around the twins.

They wrapped their arms around each other.

*"We'll go together,"* Daphna whispered. She was shivering uncontrollably.

Dex could only nod—shiver and nod.

"Where are the bodies?" a voice asked from the top of the stairs. *His* voice—suave, seductive, deadly.

"They are hiding in the basement," Brother Joe replied. "In a compartment under the steps."

At this Daphna could not suppress a sob. She felt, as she had the last time they'd hidden there, a fear that was utterly electric. Her body was going to short itself out.

"Why are they not dead!" Lilit demanded.

"My Lord!" Brother Joe pled, "I do not think they have the talismans! And the girl, she discovered me. She knows her mother is dead, so I summoned you—"

"Kill them!" Lilit roared. "Prove your loyalty to me and kill them! I will find the Aleph. I feel its energy here, like sparks."

Brother Joe didn't respond at first, but finally he choked out, "As you wish, my Lord." The twins heard him coming down the steps.

Daphna started flailing, so Dexter squeezed her tight.

But she was looking for something. *"Dex!"* she hissed in a strangled scream. *"Do you have a flashlight in here?"*

"A flashlight?"

"The Aleph! It's in *here!*" The electric current Daphna felt—it wasn't coming from inside her.

"I have to kill you," Brother Joe said. He was standing on the other side of the door, probably directly over the last person he'd murdered. "I'm sorry," he said. "You are good kids who never meant to be a part of this." The sound of the house being torn apart—this time literally—nearly downed him out.

Dex shoved his sister aside and reached for the penlight on its nail. *Of course it's in here!* he thought. *That's why Evelyn helped me hide the door. She wanted a hiding spot too!*

"I have to kill you," Brother Joe repeated.

"Hurry, Dex!"

Dexter flipped on the light and scanned the heaps of junk. *How could they find a little book in all this mess?*

"I'm sorry," Brother Joe said again. "The old abbot was my father. I was the product of a youthful indiscretion—an indiscretion his great faith in God would not let him acknowledge."

"Where is it?" Daphna screamed, her eyes darting from one piece of junk to the next.

"He didn't even know who I was when I came to the abbey. I told him, of course, just before he died. He wasted fifty years looking for a God he chose over his own child, a God who never once answered his prayers. He admitted that to me just before I crushed him in the shelves."

"I don't see it!" Dex howled.

"I came to find revenge and a God who acts in this world."

"Up! Shine it up!"

"And I found both."

There, tucked up under the bottom of one of the steps over their heads, was a makeshift shelf. On it sat a small, thin silver book. Daphna snatched it down. The cover felt like metal.

"I'm sorry."

Daphna opened the book.

There was a burst of vibrant, multihued emanations, lights like spikes reaching out in all possible ways, pointing in every direction like an infinite compass rose. Nothing was inside the book—not even pages—just the light.

The twins looked into it and saw—everything.

They saw a dark blue butterfly and a green parrot with red eyes. They saw the ash tree in the Clearing. They saw an hourglass leaking sand. They saw a blind man walking slowly through a library.

They saw the brimming ocean and every drop of water that made it up. They saw every star in the sky. They saw a pomegranate on a golden plate, a cornfield maze, steam hissing from a teapot, and a circus tent. They saw their own rib cages sheltering their throbbing hearts. They saw a hand scrape a curved rock across the page of a book. They saw a drop of red liquid fall from the tip of a knife. They saw guards at a flaming gate.

They saw themselves looking into the Aleph, and inside that Aleph they saw themselves looking into it again, and again, and again.

They saw Virgil Durante leaning over the Book of Maps in a well-appointed room. They saw men and women in crocodile and hippo masks, assembling at barricades around the Village. They saw neighborhood kids advancing on their house with bats and rakes. They saw police vehicles speeding their way. They saw Dr. Roberta Fludd in the front seat of one, watching the signal being sent by a transmitter hidden in Daphna's shoe.

"I'm sorry," said Brother Joe.

And then they saw the eye, the all-knowing, all-seeing Eye. And they saw that it was afraid.

"You have failed me," Lilit declared, just outside the door.

"Please!" begged Brother Joe. "I can help you! *El-Sham-ieen—*"

There was a cracking snap, and then the sound of a body hitting the floor.

Mesmerized, the twins reached for the light. It expanded when they touched it, filling the space under the stairs and spilling out into the basement.

Lilit smashed the door in.

But the closet was empty.

*About the Author*

David Michael Slater is an acclaimed author of books for children, teens, and adults. He teaches English to eighth graders, but you will not be required to take a test after reading this book. David lives in Reno, Nevada with his wife and son. You can learn more about David and his work at www.davidmichaelslater.com.

www.ingramcontent.com/pod-product-compliance
Lightning Source LLC
Chambersburg PA
CBHW060427260626
47161CB00005B/1823

* 9 7 8 0 9 9 8 3 3 3 4 3 4 *